I, The Spy

For Keisha,

Look! You found an adventure.

Enjoy!

I, The Spy

[signature]

Allison Maher

thistledown press

Library and Archives Canada Cataloguing in Publication

Maher, Allison, 1967-
I, the spy / Allison Maher.

ISBN-10 1-897235-04-6
ISBN-13 978-1-897235-04-1

I. Title.

PS8626.A417I116 2006   jC813'.6   C2006-900504-4

Cover and book design by Jackie Forrie
Typeset by Thistledown Press

Thistledown Press Ltd.
633 Main Street
Saskatoon, Saskatchewan, S7H 0J8
www.thistledownpress.com

Thistledown Press gratefully acknowledges the financial assistance of the Canada Council for the Arts, the Saskatchewan Arts Board, and the Book Publishing Industry Development Program of the Department of Canadian Heritage for its publishing program.

To Karen Norman, my keel. On whose strong supports all things stand. She points the way ahead and guides me, from both this world and the next.

To Jeanne Coeuille, my jib and my mainsail without which my beautiful boat becomes a simple dory. Together, we shall conquer the globe and all life's other adventures along the way.

To Cindy Charlton, my anchor and safe harbour. My first port in any storm, where calm seas and silent strength await me. I need you more than you could ever know.

To David Lee Bowlby, my magnetic North, whose magical and invisible pull, allow all my roads to lead to home; to you. More than eggs.

CONTENTS

The New Kid

For the first fifteen years of my life, I'd lied to people about what my mom does for a living and it had never been a problem. People would ask what she did. Mom would lie. Dad would lie. I would lie. We would all lie. It was never the same lie, but it worked with very few problems. It was a great system until Brian showed up.

He showed up for the spring term. At first he was just a shy new guy in my class, a little shorter than my 5' 6", with brown eyes and dark brown hair he wore in a buzz cut. His clothes didn't look like they fit very well, because he was always pulling at them. I wasn't sure if wrong-sized clothes were supposed to be fashionable where he came from, or if he had a big brother whose hand-me-downs weren't working out very well.

He never seemed too interested in talking to anybody and almost never smiled. Mostly, he stared at his feet. He seemed to be studying them, maybe hoping the answers for our math test would magically pop out of the toe of his shoe. (Not a bad plan if it works.) It was easy to tell he was from a city because he had a 'don't talk to strangers unless they talk to you first' attitude.

Here in the Annapolis Valley of Nova Scotia we have the exact opposite idea. We say hello to everyone we pass by, if we know them or not. It's the country. We're just so excited to find another human instead of another tree or cow, we just have to say hi. It's considered quite strange if you don't say *something*.

The valley is shaped like a huge rectangle. To the north and south, there are long tree-covered hills that stretch the length of the valley and there are pockets of small farms. We call these hills the North Mountain and South Mountain to make ourselves feel bigger. Each of the bumps and peaks along the North Mountain has been given their own mountain names as well.

All roads here are in a grid pattern. They either run east and west along the length of the valley or straight across from mountain to mountain. The towns run in alphabetical order down the valley floor from Auburn and Aylesford through Berwick, Cambridge, Coldbrook, Kentville, New Minas and finally end in Wolfville.

I live in the village of Aylesford, and it straddles the Annapolis River, which is usually a small stream with the exception of two weeks in the spring and one week in the fall when the rains are heavy. The village of Aylesford has thirty-one streets in total. One of the streets is called School Street even though the school was moved to Main Street forty years ago.

They added some green steel trim to the red brick exterior of the two-storey rectangle school to spruce it up. Now the tourists call it "charming" when they drive by. It only holds two hundred kids, so it's easy to know everyone there.

It took Brian a good month to start warming up to the idea of life at St. Mary's School. One day he started talking to me in class. "Please tell me Mr. Morgan will stop saying everything twice, saying everything twice. If you tell me he's going to do this all year, my brain is going to explode, going to explode."

"Mr. Morgan has a small stutter, small stutter," I explained with a smile.

Brian raised his eyebrows halfway up his forehead. "No way!" he said. "A stutter is when someone gets stuck on a sound like 'th-th-th-th those are nice t-t-t-t teeth. Do you m-m-mind getting them out of my s-s-s soup'. People can't stutter a whole sentence!"

"Wanna make a bet, wanna make a bet?" I replied, in my best Mr. Morgan voice. "Besides, after a while you won't even notice. That's when you really have to watch yourself. I've caught myself

a couple of times. When I ask him a question, sometim
to imitate his stutter and say the last half of each sentenc
It'll get you too!"

We started talking and I discovered Brian could be uncontrollably funny. He had a dry, slow humor that sneaks up on you. As
time went on and he met more people, he didn't seem to pray to
the shoe god, looking for answers to math questions, nearly as
often.

I decided to invite him to my house after school to play football.
I realize this was the moment when everything started to go off
track. Don't get me wrong. Brian and I are going to be friends
forever. We joke now and say we had a bonding experience . . . James
Bond that is.

At first everything went great.

Mom's car pulled into the driveway just as I threw the ball. We
were alternating between firing the ball directly at one another, or
aiming just far enough away to make the other run to catch it. Brian
never even put his hands up; I hit him square in the head and the
ball bounced straight up in the air. It was pretty funny that I beaned
him because he wasn't paying attention.

I laughed for a couple of seconds and waited. He didn't pick up
the ball or even move. I started walking over to him to see what was
up or to tease him maybe. "Are you all right?" I asked.

He half-turned to look at me. "Whose car is that?" he asked,
pointing at my mom's car as it was coming up the driveway.

"It's my mom's," I told him. "She's just getting home from work."

He didn't take his eyes off the car. "Why does your mom need
radio frequency tracking antennas?"

I stared at him dumbfounded. Nobody knows what radio
frequency tracking antennas look like, I thought. People have asked
me *what* was on mom's roof before. I told them all kinds of lies,
like, "They're so she can send faxes from the cellphone in her car,"
or "My Grandpa was a trucker and he gave her his antique CB
radio."

d, trying to dummy it up for me. "Why
icking equipment attached to her car?"
w do you lie to someone who knows
t? The look on Brian's face gave me the
le and dark but, at the same time, his
He was as white as death. As a stalling
ced up the forgotten ball.

Mom ... as only Mom can do, she slipped right
into the conversation as if she had been in on it all along. "You're
right. These are R.F. tracking antennas. I work for the wildlife office
and we're tracking some of the deer in the area. There is a lot of
poaching this time of year. Certain parts of the deer are worth a
lot of money if you can get them to Asia while they're fresh."

Brian stood frozen for a few more minutes as we both watched
Mom walk casually into the house and close the door behind her.
Then for the first time in a long while, he seemed to shrink and go
back to being that new kid who looked down at his shoes all the
time. No math questions necessary. I watched him in silence, in
part because of the shock over the antenna thing, and also because
his reaction was so strange I wasn't sure *what* to do.

It was as if someone had turned on a light switch. The colour
returned to Brian's face, he looked up and started moving again,
like a robot would if its computer went through a reboot cycle.
"Um, I . . . I guess I should be going home. I . . . ah, have a lot of
homework to do for tomorrow," Brian stuttered in a weak, far away
voice.

We both nodded and he grabbed his backpack and walked out
the driveway. I thought about calling him back. We didn't have any
homework for the next day. After all, we were in the same class. I
let him go though, because I had something to do. I had to talk to
Mom.

I headed for the house, but when I reached the front door, I
looked back after him. Brian was running down the street. Not a
casual jog as if he was late for something; he was really running.
Like a dog was chasing him. A big dog at that.

Mom looked past my shoulder when I came in. "Where's you friend?" she asked.

I told her he had gone home, and I sat down to join her for a cup of Dad's famously bad homemade, organic iced tea. "That was weird out there. I didn't know what to say. How did you come up with the Department of Lands and Forest thing so fast?"

"It takes practice and unfortunately I've have plenty of practice," said Mom with a shrug of her shoulders and a sigh.

"But how would Brian know what the antennas were on your car, and why would he act *so* strange when he saw them?"

"Well . . . " Mom said slowly. I could imagine the wheels turning in her head as she picked up her peppermint iced tea and took a sip. If she started pulling on her eyebrows, I knew I would lose her. She would pull on her eyebrows and drift off into her own little world whenever she had a problem to figure out. It was a sign of extreme concentration.

"Mom? Maybe Brian's dad uses spy gear for one of the police agencies?"

"No, no, no," she said, flitting her hand back and forth like she was swatting flies. "If he knew someone who used our gear he'd be more than familiar with how we hide the antennas than with what they look like out in the open. Criminals are getting smarter these days."

"Here we go," I thought out loud, "Mom and her *very familiar* speech about *tell-all TV*."

Her voice started to rise, "All those ridiculous real-life crime shows are making it harder for the police to do their jobs. They keep showing the police setting up equipment on undercover cars. Now even the stupidest criminals know what they look like, so now *we* have to come up with ways to hide the antennas inside things like ski racks or the light bar on top of taxis."

"Maybe Brian is one of those junior sleuth guys and saw a police car all set up with tracking antennas in a magazine and remembers it," I offered trying to cut her off.

"Could be," Mom said, but I knew neither of us believed it. "Maybe you should invite him over for supper and we can *all* get to know him a little better."

"Does it mean we have to clean the house up like we do when Grandma and Grandpa are coming for the holidays?"

"What do you mean?"

"You know. When you run around and hide everything that looks like electronics, diagrams or manuals and stuff it all into closets and laundry hampers. Then when Grandma and Grandpa go home we all spent the next three days trying to find the gym shorts you used to wrap antennas with, before you shoved them into the bottom of the freezer to hide them. All so Grandma won't accidentally find something?"

She smiled a crooked smile, "I didn't think you ever noticed." Mom took one look at my shocked face and laughed.

In our house, just about everything we've ever owned has fallen victim to something Mom was working on. We always have speaker wires, black steel boxes, battery packs, mini satellite dishes or extra antennas stuck to the car, or the side of the house.

More often than not, that included me. Every time Mom needed to test another piece of equipment to see how far the signal could carry, she would send me out of the house with it and tell me to walk away with the transmitter held over my head. Not a normal thing to do, especially when you can't tell anyone *why* you're doing it.

"Honey, it's all right, I'm on the side of the good guys, remember. The sky is not falling. Brian's a smart kid who watched the right TV show and remembers it, that's all."

Secret, Secret,
Who Has A Secret!

Brian didn't come to school again until Thursday. When he did show up, he walked right over to me and started talking.

"Where have you been?" I asked.

"Oh . . . I've been sick. My mom thought I should stay at home for a few days until I got better." After a brief glance at his shoes and a shrug, he smiled at me again.

Mom had been asking me every day if I had invited Brian over for supper yet. It was starting to make me nervous. I liked him a lot, and I was a little worried about what my mother was planning for him. She hadn't shown this much interest in anything since the miniature mouth transmitter accident.

Someone she works with had thought up the idea of taking a string of watch batteries and connecting them with a mini transmitter. It was supposed to sit under your lip, in the space where you hide gum if the teacher asks what's in your mouth. They dropped the idea of an *in-your-mouth* transmitter shortly after Mom gave it to me, to test. After I accidentally swallowed it, Mom followed me around for days asking if I was all right. She had that same eagerness now as she was asking me about Brian.

Mr. Morgan assigned a math project on Brian's first day back. We were partners and he was back to being his old funny self. In fact, he was even funnier than usual. I thought we were going to get kicked out of class. Brian had a sneaky smile on his face. "OK, why do rabbits hate math."

"I have no idea but my guess is I'm about to find out."

Brian could barely hold himself down as he delivered the punch line. "Because they can't eat square roots!"

We never even came close to finishing our project. It made a perfect opening and I really did like Brian, so I took a deep breath, reassured myself that everything was going to be all right and asked him if he wanted to come over for supper tomorrow night.

He looked at me with a sparkle of humour in his eyes. "Sure man, sure man," he joked. "I bet Mr. Morgan has second helpings of everything. Could I have a piece of pie, could I have a piece of pie?

We both laughed.

"Please don't let me keep stuttering when we get to your house," Brian continued, "I'm trying to diet so I only want to eat it once!"

"No problem there. Dad's an environmental biologist *and* the cook in our house. He's always dragging home some weird thing he's found in the woods for us to eat. The first time anyone eats over they *never* have seconds. My parents and I even take bets on it."

"Come on man," said Brian. "Everyone thinks they have the weirdest parents. Yours can't be that bad."

That night at dinner, Brian kept his eye on Mom but it was Dad who did almost all the talking.

"You know Brian, I've lived here all my life. It must be interesting moving around like you have. Tell me, where's the nicest place you've ever lived?"

"I guess it would be Aylesford," Brian said with his eyebrows raised up almost enough to meet his hairline. "Everyone is so friendly. People you meet on the sidewalk say hi for no reason. We were at the supermarket once when we first arrived and this lady walked over to my dad to show him how much fat was on the bacon and complain about it. It was like we were supposed to do something. It's enough to make a person paranoid. These people keep appearing out of nowhere to talk to you."

"People aren't as friendly where you used to live?" Dad asked.

"It was Chicago!" Brian exclaimed. He was looking at Dad like he had ten heads "Hollywood doesn't make Chicago the home of the bad guys in all their movies for nothing. Name one movie you've seen where the mob is from Nashville or Cleveland."

Dad laughed out loud. "I guess you are right. Funny, but I'd heard your family was from Detroit."

"Oh yeah, I guess we've lived there too," Brian said a little too fast.

"I've never been to Detroit," Dad started to say. Then he eased in for the kill. I had been caught in his traps before and could see them coming. "They say the Golden Gate Bridge is beautiful. I've heard it's quite a landmark, right in the middle of the city. You must have driven over it hundreds of times. Is it really painted gold?"

I could feel it coming. I froze in mid-chew so I could listen without the crunch of food between my teeth. It was as if time had stopped for a split second. Dad and Mom had chosen that exact same moment to butter a slice of bread.

"Yeah man," Brian answered. "It's all painted in a gold colour and glows like the sun. I'm surprised the mob guys don't try to cut it up and steal it."

Dad put his slice of bread carefully on the side of his plate, looked straight at Brian and waited. When they finally made eye contact, Dad held his gaze to make sure he had Brian's full attention. "Brian, the Golden Gate Bridge is in San Francisco and to most people's surprise, the bridge is not even a little bit golden.

"Please don't be upset, Brian. Every family has their own secrets. Heavens knows we have enough of our own but I want you to know, without question, you and your secret are safe. You don't have to lie to us."

Brian's eyes grew huge as he straightened up in his chair. He glanced quickly at the table, then turned his head toward the door. Even I knew he was thinking about making a run for it.

"There are very few people in the world that would have recognized the antennas on my car the way you did. I know you've spent some time on the *right* side of the law," Mom said. "We're on the right side too. You know that because you know what's on the roof of my car. You are safe here. Is there anything you might like to tell us?"

Brian was silently staring at his plate. I could tell by the changing expressions on his face, Brian was trying to work things out. I glanced at Mom and she signaled me to sit still and wait.

Sure enough, Brian started to talk. In fact he talked and he talked and he talked. "I'm not allowed to tell anybody the truth," he blurted out. "I keep forgetting the story they made us practice. I hate lying to people all the time and I'm always afraid I'll slip up and then we'll have to move again. When we first moved here, I thought it would be easier if I didn't talk to anyone at all. My folks said I had to 'get on with my life'. It seems like I slip up every day and say something that's the truth and then I worry about it for weeks after. Sometimes I get so confused about what lies I've told and who I've told them to."

"I've always lived in Chicago. Dad worked for this company and something went wrong. One day I was in school and Mom came to pick me up early. She was acting funny and her face was white, like she was sick. She kept touching me, hugging me and at the same time telling me to hurry.

"When we left the school, there was a black car out front," he continued, "We walked up to it, these guys got out and opened the back doors and Mom climbed right in like she had done it a hundred times before. When I asked what was going on, she told me to please hurry and that everything was going to be all right."

He looked thoughtful for a moment. "She was wrong. Everything has been wrong ever since I got into the big black car. I never got to say goodbye to any of my friends. I didn't get to take my own clothes, and it doesn't seem to matter what I buy anymore, it never fits right." Almost to demonstrate, he pulled and stretched at the sleeves of his shirt.

"Then there's my library book. When Mom took me out of school that day, I had a library book in my backpack. It was supposed to be an overnight release only. It's been over six months!

What kind of late charge do you suppose I owe on it?" Even stressed and upset, Brian could find room to make a joke.

I started to ask who was in the black car that took Brian and his family away but Dad signaled me to be quiet. I guess he knew this meeting wasn't over yet. There were a few moments of silence.

"Brian," Mom said quietly, "I don't want you to feel bad because of what you've told us. Most people, especially honest ones, *want to* confess. How many people don't know the expression 'and the truth shall set you free?'"

"My dad didn't do anything illegal," Brian stated. "This shouldn't be happening to us."

"You're right, it isn't fair," Mom confirmed.

Brian looked up at the three of us, eyeing us all slowly. "They put us into the Witness Protection Program. My real name is Brian Fiske and you probably read about my dad last year in the newspapers. He *was* Keith Fiske, the famous mob buster. Now you know who I am, and who we are."

Keith Fiske, The Spy

Keith Fiske worked for a trading company, based in Chicago, with branches all over the world. He handled paper trails, such as cash transfers.

One day after work as Keith walked through the car park, a van pulled up beside him and three men jumped out flashing badges. "FBI, Mr. Fiske. Would you mind stepping into the van?" Keith thought it seemed an odd thing for these men to ask, as they were practically picking him up and *putting* him in the van. The door slammed behind him, before he had a chance to protest.

"Hey boys," Keith said, in what he hoped would be a strong voice. "Umm . . . Whatever it is, I'm sure you have the wrong man."

"I assure you Mr. Fiske, we do not have the wrong man," said the man closest to him. "We mean you no harm, but it will be much safer for you if we wait until we get to the compound to talk."

"What do you mean *compound*?" Keith demanded.

The same man spoke up again. "Please sir, it's only a few more minutes."

After twenty minutes of dead silence the van slowed down and turned to enter an underground garage. It stopped in front of the garage door, and the driver cut the engine.

Two men, who looked like gardeners, stepped up to the van and began to circle it. Keith watched as the one who was holding an odd-looking electric broom device, passed it over and under the van. The other man was holding a black paddle with a little red light on the end. He seemed to be waving it all over the place. When they were finished, the two men simply walked away.

Before he had a chance to ask any questions, the talkative fellow spoke up. He explained the security guards were doing a visual ID on the people in the van and an electronics sweep on the van to make sure everything was all right.

They started through a maze of a building. Everywhere they went they had to use different security keys, credit cards keys and security codes punched into keypads. The longer they walked, the more frightened Keith became. Whatever this was, it was serious.

The journey finally came to a stop when they dropped him off at the door of a small room, barely big enough to hold the large table in the middle. All but one of the ten chairs had someone already sitting in it. There were no windows either, but Keith knew right away the giant mirror on one wall was not for checking his hair. He had seen enough police shows to know a two-way mirror when he saw one.

He sank down in the remaining empty chair.

They started to talk. Keith tried to look into their eyes but the longer they talked the more he knew, with a sinking feeling, he was in serious trouble now. He stared at his feet and listened.

The FBI explained how money moves around the country, and the world, in certain patterns. It moves south in the winter with people who vacation to get away from the cold and north again in the summer, when people who live in the south head north to avoid the heat.

In the fall, when farmers are making money, it flows in from the prairies, and ends up in Chicago. At Christmastime, stores are making money. It flows in and ends up in New York. There are hundreds of these patterns and they are very easy to track. They never change. So when counterfeit money starts showing up in the system, they can figure out where it came from.

By using different math formulas and keeping track of where the money shows up, they can tell where counterfeit money is being released. The FBI had tracked one such counterfeit operation all the way back to the company Keith worked for. They knew Keith was the one moving most of these bills. They told him it was called laundering and he could go to prison for it.

The sinking feeling he had earlier was gone. Keith felt hot and cold at the same time. He'd been the one in charge of laundering hundreds of thousands in counterfeit money. He'd known that there was something odd about the money that passed through his office, but he never questioned it. It was a great job and he didn't want to lose it.

They needed an insider to help catch the organization running the whole thing, and Keith was the person who could help them the most. Whether he wanted to join the poker game or not, his hand was already dealt in — he was their man.

Keith heard a small, weak voice coming from somewhere inside him. "But I have a wife and a teenage boy. What are you going to do with them?"

"If you are successful in helping us, we will put your family into the witness protection program and you can start a new life. Anywhere but here," said a small person from the far side of the table.

Keith couldn't tell whether the person who had answered his question had been a man, or a woman. He/she was wearing a straight-cut, black suit, ordinary eyeglasses and had short brown hair.

"If I'm going to have to work with you people to make this happen, could you at least tell me your names? You know mine," Keith said.

"No. I am sorry, Mr. Fiske. After today, the only person you will be in contact with is going to be agent Pat Charlton," explained an older man, who had been quiet up until this point. He seemed like someone who was in charge. "Pat will bring you up to speed on everything you will need to know. If you have any question, ask Pat."

Keith nodded in agreement.

For the next two hours, Pat showed Keith where to wear a microphone located on a miniature voice transmitter. Close to his head, not down by his feet. Pat showed him how batteries get hot when they were worked hard, so you had to try to keep them away from your skin.

Pat was the only person Keith saw on the way out.

The next day Keith went to work with his cheat notes from the FBI on who he should talk to and what to ask them. Pat had told him what to copy, what to fax and what to e-mail.

Ten minutes after he had finished he started walking out of his office and toward a new life in Canada. He knew there were thirty armed police officers watching the building from various locations, both outside and inside. They were all waiting for the signal to move in.

The signal was Keith leaving. He had been nervous and shaking the entire time he was in his office. Now he was beginning to sweat. He could feel the damp hair on the back of his neck and his sweat covered palms. When he was close enough to see the front doors ahead of him, he stopped to take a last look around. Keith had enjoyed working here. Most of these people had become friends.

Every fibre in his body was tingling and his mouth was dry. Keith knew if he didn't start moving again he was going to faint. Taking a deep breath, he willed himself to start walking. He barely felt the door in his hand as he pushed it open. The air outside wrapped itself around him. He was grateful for its cool cleansing touch.

Keith began to count his strides.

Three paces outside the front door, Keith noticed a group of overdressed businessmen begin to move toward the building, as if on cue. The hot dog vender dropped his apron, picked up a bag and headed toward the building too.

At ten strides two black vans burst open and heavily armed men in black riot gear spilled out like a terrifying flood, and charged past him toward the front door.

At twenty-two strides, half a dozen police cars turned on their sirens. The sound screamed through his brain like a liquid fire. Keith could not force himself to walk one more step. Against what he had been told to do, Keith broke into a run. Maybe he was running *for* his life? Maybe he was running *to* his life?

Behind the Mask

Everyone was quiet for a long time. People think the opposite of noise is quiet. They are wrong. This was more like negative noise, where any sound that should have been in the room seemed to stop, and decide to go back where it came from, or get sucked up in a huge vacuum of anti-noise.

Brian was sitting very still, with his head tilted back and his hands relaxed in his lap. He stared blankly off into space with a half-smile and eyes that said, '*don't talk to me 'cause nobody is home.*'

I kept waiting for him to turn back into the guy who loved to stare at his sneakers, but it didn't seem as if that was going to happen. I didn't want to startle him, or scare him so without moving my head, I shifted my eyes to look at Mom and Dad. I didn't think I'd get the look that says, "Just you wait until I get you alone. Boy are you going to have some explaining to do!" It wasn't my fault I brought home the son of the most famous mob-buster. At least I hoped not.

Mom had one hand flat on the table beside the plate she had pushed away while Brian was talking. The other hand was under her chin with her elbow resting on the table. Her fingers were positioned near her eyebrow as if ready to start stroking them. This time her fingers were perfectly still. Her eyes had turned a dark grey and were locked like cold iron on Dad's face.

Dad had also magically pushed away his plate when I wasn't looking. With both elbows resting on the table, his arms made a triangle shape with his chin soundly placed at the top of his fists. Unlike Mom, his eyes were peaceful and calm. He stared back at

Mom as if the two of them were having a conversation and the rest of the world was not allowed to listen. Simply looking at him made me feel better. Nothing ever ruffled Dad's feathers.

Brian was the first to move. He took a deep breath and started to talk. "Sounds pretty crazy doesn't it? It's okay if you don't believe me. I know I wouldn't if someone told me they were in the Witness Protection Program. I guess it doesn't honestly matter if you believe me or not.

Once they find out I've told you who we were, they'll pack us up and move us again." He paused but didn't look up so we all kept silent and waited some more. "I guess that's what they'll do . . . Maybe. Oh man, are my folks ever going to be mad!"

"Now don't get carried away," Dad said finally. I could tell he was trying to calm Brian down because he reached over and squeezed his hand. Dad looked back at Mom and she nodded her head and stood up.

"Actually Brian, we all believe you. Perhaps it's time we share a few of our secrets with you." Mom winked at me. I think she fought off a smile.

"Come on, boys," Dad said. "How about we let Andrew's mom make some phone calls while we finish eating supper? Then you two can do the dishes and tidy up, while I put on a pot of coffee and call Brian's parents. Its time we sat down and had a long talk."

Brian started to look confused and a little suspicious. "Please Mr. Johnston. Don't call my parents yet! I have to go home and tell them what I've done."

"Look Brian," Dad said, "You picked the right place to spill the beans. I'd like to think you knew you'd be safe here. Always trust your instincts, son. They'll help keep you out of trouble and they didn't fail you this time. I promise you're not going to get into trouble over this. You can let it go."

He left no room for argument. "Come on and eat up. I tried extra hard to make this a *normal* meal."

Mom had already slipped away from the table. We didn't see her again for two hours. By the time she came back up out of her office/cave in the basement the Lutzs had arrived.

We were sitting in the living room. The parents were chatting the very polite just-met-you speak, when a strange man came into the room through the hallway from the back door. He was dressed in a black spandex jogging suit that covered everything from the tips of his toes to the top of his head. The only thing that was exposed was his face as he pulled back his black hood. He even had black spandex gloves on.

"Marion," he said nodding his head toward Brian's mother. Then he turned to Brian's dad, who was now standing. "Nice to see you again, Keith. I trust your new house is everything you had hoped."

"I can explain!" yelled Brian as he jumped to his feet, recognizing the man. He tried to put himself between his parents and this sneaky guy in black who had managed to slither his way into the house.

Dad stepped forward with the relaxing and peaceful air he's so good at. He took both of Brian's parents by the hand and sat them back down. "I believe we all know one another," he said turning to include the man in black.

I couldn't believe it. How would my dad know this guy? What were the chances of the sneaky guy knowing Brian's parents as well? I started feeling a little out of the ball game. "I don't know him or how he got into the house!" I called out.

"This isn't about you Andrew," Mom said firmly, giving me the look to shut up. "You didn't expect someone like him to come up to the front door and knock, did you?"

Dad turned to Brian's parents. "I'm sorry for the surprise but we thought this might be easier for you to believe, if we had a more formal introduction. We called NAIPA earlier this evening and they promised to send one of the area agents over. I see you've met Don Proctor before," he said, indicating his head toward the man in black.

Everyone nodded in unison except me. "What the heck is NAIPA?" I demanded. I was ignored.

"We don't know all the details of why you're in the witness protection program, and you don't have to tell us anything. We arranged this so you'd know we're being honest in our attempt to help you with the changes you're going through. We thought if someone from NAIPA introduced us, then you'd know we're on the side of the good guys."

The NAIPA agent took over and told the Lutzs it was safe at our house and that we had offered to help his agency with the Fiske relocation case as they eased into becoming the Lutz family.

Mom asked Brian's mother and father if there was anything special they were having a hard time adjusting to. Mrs. Lutz said she was worried about Grandma Fiske; she just wanted to talk to her and say they were all fine.

Mom nodded to Agent Proctor. He nodded back and they both took the Lutz family into the basement and let them use the phone in Mom's office. I followed. Grabbing Brian by the elbow I asked, "What's a NAIPA?"

"It stands for North American Integrated Policing Agency," explained Brian. They're the guys who talk back and forth over the Canada and US border." He then turned his attention back to Agent Proctor.

"Although we have told you that you may never contact anyone from your old life *ever* again," lectured the agent. "This will be the one exception. There is no way to trace a call back to this phone. It has an electronic version of an old fashion 'party line' where more than one house shared a phone line. Each house had a different number and ring so you knew when to answer. With this electronic version, if someone tried to get a trace on the phone, they would get different locations in Greenland, Germany and New York City.

"Remember not to talk about what it looks like, the weather or politics. Everything you say can be used by whoever is listening, to help them find you. For example if you said 'the mountains were beautiful yesterday when it was snowing. We got six inches of it and because the Liberal Party is trying to save money, we didn't get plowed out until after supper'.

"From that sentence alone the bad guys have a fairly good chance of finding you.

"The first thing they learned is you live in Canada and not the United States because you said Liberal Party, as in Canada, and not Republican or Democrat, as in the USA.

"The second thing they would know is you live near the mountains. They would look at the three or four major mountain ranges in Canada and find out which ones had a major snowfall, between four and eight inches, on that date.

"Thirdly, they could then narrow it down even further, because they know it must have been snowing between 7:00 AM and 6:00 PM. You said you could see the snow falling on the mountains. You can't see mountaintops at night, so it must have been snowing during the daytime. Local newspapers usually report the times of sunrise and sunset. This time of year, dawn is at seven, and dusk is at six.

"The fourth thing they could look at is finding out which of these areas had Liberal Governments, instead of any of the other political parties.

"Once they get it narrowed down that far, they could call the Department of Highways office and say they are doing an article for the newspaper and need to find out which areas had been plowed after supper. From there they could narrow it down to only a few streets and BANG they have you."

Keeping these things in mind, the Lutz family was allowed to call their friends and family back home. They spent the next half-hour reassuring everyone they were all right.

When they weren't on the phone we were all in the living room trading stories about our secret lives. It felt great to be able to tell Brian all about helping Mom test tracking equipment, recording devices and body alarms. Everything was always so hush-hush. Even if I had been allowed to talk about it, I didn't know anyone who would have understood *any* of it.

While they had been moving around in the witness protection program, Brian had been allowed to see, and fiddle with, some of the exact same equipment. We tried to compare it to Mom's stuff we had in the house.

I asked if it would be okay if I showed Brian some of Mom's homework. Mom said I could. We stayed up half the night playing around with the electronics in the basement. Some of it was older gear that used only radio to communicate, but most of it used GPSs (Global Positioning Systems), cellular telephones, and satellite interface, ultraviolet or infrared.

It was wonderful having someone I could be completely honest with.

Dial M for Mob

B y the end of the school year, I thought Brian was starting to like living here. His nervous habit of shoe staring only popped up around pretty girls. He even managed to buy summer clothes that fit him.

We were inseparable. When we weren't sneaking Mom's tracking transmitters and voice transmitters out of the office to play electronic hide and seek, we were hanging out with the rest of the kids in town. They seemed to like Brian. We went to the movies, played video games, ate pizza and generally hung out, the same as teenagers everywhere. It was a great year.

The unwritten rule between Brian and I was, when other people were around we didn't talk about our little tricks and the secret games we were playing. We both knew that when you try to talk over people's heads, they feel left out and end up getting ticked off at you.

I don't need any of my other friends thinking I'm any weirder than they already do. They've come to expect my family to be a little off as it is. At my age, trying to fit in is the rule.

Early the next September, Brian was standing in front of my locker when I arrived at school. "I have to talk to you later," he said. "So don't forget to come and find me after the last bell."

I didn't think anything about it. In fact, I never thought about it again until Brian came up behind me. "Hey man! Wait up. I have to tell you something.

"Look man, I'm either going crazy or getting paranoid." He continued, "It's probably nothing. Maybe I'm feeling overrun with minivans. I know we live in the country and you can't go to the opera for entertainment, but *how many* people can get satellite TV hooked up in *one* week? Is it a plague of boredom?"

"What are you talking about?"

"The satellite TV repair van. Its been sitting somewhere on my street for the past week. Nobody has a receiver that gets so messed up it takes a week to fix it!"

"Dad always says to trust your instincts," I told him. "Maybe you should tell the NAIPA people right away."

Brian scowled at me hard through his downward pressed eyebrows. "Tell them what? I think there's an evil looking minivan lurking around? They'll take one *noid* out of my left pocket and pull another *noid* out of my right pocket and hold them under my nose and say 'look kid, we found your *pair-of-noids*. Now go home and be a messed up little teenager.' Instincts?" he huffed. "I don't know if it's my instincts or gas. *Maybe* I should just try passing some wind. Then I'd feel better about this whole thing."

"You might feel better, but I sure wouldn't," I joked. "No, you can keep your gas to yourself!"

Brian perked up. "We could bug my house with some of your mom's stuff. Maybe set up some of her motion detector alarms. You know, man, wire the house and yard so we can tell if anyone has been sneaking around when we're not there."

"All right, after school we'll go raid Mom's office big time. She hasn't finished testing the voice transmitter so I know we still have it at least. We have a GPS tracking transmitter too. I knocked it into the bathroom sink a while back. Mom hasn't gotten around to cleaning it up enough to bring it back to work."

"I don't know, man," he said. "I feel a little better, but I've still got this creepy feeling inside. Kind of like butterflies having a fist fight." Brian seemed to relax a bit, and smiled thoughtfully. "This is good. Yes, this is good. Okay it's a plan. We'll do it after school."

Three hours later we were gathering electronics from around the house. You never realize how much stuff you have until you have to gather it, or count it. Take your locker for example. At the beginning of the year it has four or five books, a pencil case and your coat. By the end of the year, you need a hockey bag and a U-haul to get all your stuff home. It happens gradually. Over time your few odds and ends turn into a full-blown collection.

My parents are the worst. Last year it happened with chicken noodle soup. I mentioned we were out. For the next month, every time Mom or Dad went to the store they picked up a half dozen of cans of chicken noodle soup. We ended up with twenty-seven cans of it. Don't get me wrong. I like chicken noodle soup. However, if they stopped buying any more new cans right now, *and* even if I ate a can per week, it would take me half a year to finish it all. Now I know the reason for expiration dates on canned goods. It's to stop pack rats.

Mom is the worst pack rat of them all. I didn't realize how much of her electronic stuff was floating around our house, until I started to gather it up. The living room seemed like a good place to pile it all. Once it was all collected, we could figure out what we needed. Even Brian was amazed.

Brian looked around the room. "Doesn't your mom's boss ever notice that, like, half the shop is missing?"

"I guess not," I laughed. "It's like a Nintendo factory in there. It doesn't seem to matter how much work they put into making something. There is always another generation, or model, coming down the pipe. A bigger, better, faster, kind of thing. That's why Mom has so many of each thing. She needs matched sets of each generation of equipment, to be able to test it."

By this time Brian was trying on night vision goggles. "Radio Shack doesn't have this much stuff," he said, with what I think was a smile. It's hard to smile when you have a three-pound set of night vision goggles squeezing your cheeks down. He looked like a basset hound.

We only had an hour or so before my folks would be home, so we got out a pen and some paper to make a plan. We knew we'd need motion detector alarms, a body alarm, a disguised tracking transmitter for a car, and a voice transmitter we could plant in the house somewhere.

If we put a motion detector in the front hallway, and one by the back door, we'd cover most of the main floor of the house for any movement. Anytime one detects movement it sends a signal back to the computer with the time the movement occurred. Mom's home computer is set up to listen for transmission signals 24/7. If we check the program each night, it would tell us there was a lot of movement around seven in the morning with nothing again until three o'clock, when Brian gets home. If there are signals in between those times, we'll know someone was in the house.

Most people go to bed between eleven and twelve o'clock at night. They don't usually get up and start getting newspapers and making coffee until six. If there is a signal in the house between those hours, it would prove someone had been in there who shouldn't have been.

Maybe Brian's dad would need a body alarm. It would have to be disguised. The first thing *Bad Guys* do is throw away cellphones so their victims can't simply call for help when they aren't looking. They will take anything away from their victims if they think it will help their victim get away, but they don't generally strip them down to their Jockeys. Mom had four personal alarms sitting in a box beside her computer. One looked like a pager, two disguised as pens and one was inside a silver locket.

A pen seemed like the best answer. It looked like those old fashioned pens with the two different colours of ink. When the blue button is pressed, a pen comes out. It will even write. If the red button is pressed, the transmitter will send out one radio beep every five minutes. They are powered by watch batteries and I made sure ours was loaded with fresh ones. Even then it will only last about thirty-six hours.

Transmitters that are designed to go on vehicles are built tough. Sometimes the people being tracked are driving through snow, or the desert, or off road through a bush or swamp. The transmitters have to be watertight, temperature resistant, small and really, really sturdy. "We build a brick and put a transmitter inside it," is how Mom describes them.

The problem is, neither one of us had our driver's license, so we couldn't actually follow Keith's car anywhere. We picked the Cadillac of tracking. It uses a GPS, a small computer with a modem and a cellular telephone.

When you first turn it on the GPS system looks up at the sky and counts satellites. The satellites tell the GPS head exactly where it is and what time it is. The head gives the information to the computer, which sends it through a cellphone to a second telephone and computer system.

There are many different computerized mapping programs available. Some can take in information and do live tracks, or process each piece of information as it comes in. Still others need to wait until all the information is complete. Once you are finished tracking it will tell you where you have been and not where you are.

Brian and I chose live tracking as the best option for us. Why chase his dad on our bikes while balancing cellphones on our heads and laptop computers on our handlebars? Maybe if we were circus monkeys we could put a couple of banana milkshakes in our socks so we would have a drink when we got thirsty!

We decided it was easier to sit downstairs in Mom's office, and eat seaweed bran cookies, while watching his dad drive to work and back on the computer screen. So if his dad's car went someplace it wasn't supposed to, (like Iowa) we would at least know where he was.

The mini voice transmitter, or body wire, was easy. Brian picked one that was hidden inside a baseball hat. Brian's dad was a fan of ball caps. He called them an 'insta-poo', as in *insta*nt sham*poo*. He said it was faster to put a hat on than it was to wash your hair.

We tested everything to make sure it would work. It was time for my folks to show up. Brian put the hat on his head and packed the rest into his knapsack.

We had decided the best plan was to head over to my house every day after school to check in on the equipment. It was agreed: at the first sign of anything, or anyone, being out of place, we would go straight to Brian's parents.

One Bad Night

Six figures moved slowly along the ground across a long field toward the house, aiming for the backyard. Each was dressed in black, from the top of the head, to the bottom of the feet. Their faces had been covered with a greasy, dull, black paint.

Even the whites of the eyes were covered. They had unusual black goggles, which fit tightly on their faces. Each pair was fitted with silver bands around the frames and a small switch, right between their eyes. When they were fifty yards away from the house, they looked from one to the other, and switched on their night vision.

They covered the last stretch of ground commando style, as they crawled on their bellies on the grass. Each movement of their arms made their bodies bend and their heads sweep from side to side so they could take a long, slow look from left to right: eyes open and senses on alert for any possible movement from the neighbouring houses.

If it had been daylight, they would have looked just like lizards crawling through the tall grass. They traveled in a tight pack until they were within ten feet of the house. Then they all spread out. Keeping on their bellies, they slithered along the foundation of the house until they reached their positions.

Once in place, they set to work. They opened the Velcro pouches on the outside of their black vests. The lizards along the side of the house used explosive plastics to start with. Each squeezed a small bead of explosives in long strips under the edge of the siding.

Each of them pulled a large spray can out of another pouch and sprayed as much of the surface of the house as they could cover. The chemicals inside the can were sulfur-based and once ignited were impossible to put out. They could even burn under water.

The last piece to their puzzle was a small electrical charge, with a timer. The charges were all made with a soft plastic casing that would burn easily and completely. The lizards wanted to leave no clues behind once their work was finished. When everything was in place, they got back into lizard position, on their bellies, and lay as close to the house as they could, waiting for the others to finish.

One of the lizards slithered his way to the front porch. It took him the longest to get into place, because of all the scanning of the street and the neighbour's windows. He needed to be sure he would not be seen.

Once in place, he began his work. His first job was to make sure no one could either leave or enter the house through the front door. He pulled out an industrial size tube of contact cement and began cementing the door all the way around. He finished by filling in the keyhole.

The explosive plastic was pressed tightly along the outside of the support beams down close to the base. The beams held up the roof of the porch. Once the support beams were blown out, the roof would fall inwards over the front of the house, like a huge wood curtain. Even with the front door open, or front window smashed out, the collapsed porch roof would make it impossible to escape.

Each charge had its own timer.

He finished up by taking his can of sulfur spray and emptying most of it under the windows, with a little squirt here and there. Then he made his way off the porch and lay still in the bushes to the side of the porch. He kept a close eye on the neighbourhood, to make sure there was no movement.

At the back of the house, another lizard set explosives and sulfur spray around the kitchen and basement windows. A third went straight to work using the special tools he had tucked deep in his pockets. His black gloved hand slid into a pocket for the briefest of moments and reemerged with a diamond tipped slip knife; sharp enough for surgery and strong enough to cut glass. He handled it with skill and respect.

The quickest flick into a second pocket produced a large suction cup with a black plastic handle. In a smooth motion he attached the suction cup halfway up the window beside the back door. Then he used the slip knife to cut a circle in the glass around the suction cup. After three or four passes around the circle, he gave the handle on the suction cup a solid jerk and, almost silently, the glass came free.

The lizard slipped a hand in through the hole and unlocked the door. The other hand reached down and tested the outside doorknob. It turned freely and the bolt slid back out of the lock easily. He pulled against the door to check its resistance and to check if there was a second bolt system to keep the door secured. There was none and the door eased open a fraction of an inch. With the slightest pull, the door would simply open wide.

Pressing himself flat against the outside wall, he pushed his right hand to his chest to turn on his headset. With one word he was able to tell the other lizards everything was ready.

Each lizard then programmed timers on the explosives to go off in four minutes. Like an evil shadow, they all began to slither toward the back of the house. Once they were all together they crouched outside the back door.

The countdown began immediately.

"Ten." They all stood.

"Nine, eight, seven." They made two lines, side by side.

"Six, five, four." They all turned on their night vision goggles.

"Three, two, one." They checked their gear and leaned forward.

"Go!" The man threw open the door and the others flooded inside. They knew exactly where they were going. They also knew there were bound to be alarms, but for this operation alarms didn't matter. By the time the first one went off, they would already be deep inside. It would be too late for the victims to react. By the time the alarm sounded at the police station, or elsewhere, everyone would be on the way back outside.

They heard the first blast as the first man hit the bottom of the stairs. It sounded like a heavy book being thrown at the outside wall. The second blast went off before he reached the landing at the top. The next thump happened as Keith reached the doorway to his bedroom. A fast and silent blow to the side of his neck knocked him out immediately. The one who struck the blow charged forward into the bedroom, leaving two others coming behind him, to catch the falling man. He never touched the floor.

Marion had stayed in bed while Keith got up to see what had caused the noises. She did not struggle as they slipped the mask over her face. A second lizard went into the bedroom to help carry her out.

Brian's room was at the far end of the hall. He was fully awake and had jumped out of bed. He tried to think of a place to hide. In the dark and panic, Brian had realized all too clearly what was about to happen. His instincts told him to take the bag. In the seconds it took for the figures in black to go from his parent's room to his, Brian had slipped both of his arms through the shoulder straps of his backpack. Once they were in place, he quickly clicked together the two additional support straps around his chest. They found him standing in the middle of the room, frozen with fear, wearing pajamas and a backpack. He didn't resist one bit. He accepted his fate as they reached out for him and slipped a mask over his head.

By the time the men had carried the Lutz family out the back door, the entire outside of the house was in flames. The final explosion came when they were a few feet away. The larger charges went off at the front of the house. The blast echoed and bounced off the walls of the surrounding buildings and was quickly followed by the crunching and screaming of the wood giving way as the porch roof caved in.

With two men carrying each member of the Lutz family, one by the shoulders and one by their knees, they raced across the field toward the two vans waiting on the far side. The headlights were off, but the engines purred deep and low as they waited with the side doors open and welcoming. The lizards never even broke their strides as the thumping of their feet on the ground changed into the clang of hard-soled boots on bare metal as they ran jumped into the vans, still carrying their unconscious cargo. The metal doors slammed behind them and the engines roared as the driver sped away.

The vans started to drive away at the same time the first neighbour ran out of his house to help. With eyes locked on Brian's family's home no one noticed the vans driving away.

Sirens

About one o'clock that night, the big fire alarm went off at the fire station. I heard the long slow howl, but the trucks didn't seem to be coming in our direction, so I tried to go back to sleep. Later, when I heard more trucks, I knew they must have been coming in from the next town over. If they were calling in for reinforcements from other towns it meant a huge fire.

When the fire alarm goes off in a small town like this, everyone knows about it. Most of the time people will head over to see if they can lend a hand.

Dad called for me to get up, but I was already half dressed. We followed the sound of the fire engines, until we could see the flames and smoke. It was the biggest fire I'd ever seen in my life. I stopped walking and stared at the roaring wall of flames.

Dad kept walking toward an older fellow who was standing on the sidewalk ahead of us. "Hello George," he called. "How are they doing?"

"They're never gonna save this one!" the old man says.

"What do you think started it?" Dad asked.

"Hard to say," George said slowly. "When I was in the fire department we usually named fires by where they started. There are kitchen fires and chimney fires and garage fires. This, I would say, is a full-blown house fire. Look," he said, pointing at the front of the house, "it stretches from the grass, right up to the sky."

Flames were bursting through the shingles in five or six different places. The wraparound porch had completely given in to the fire and had collapsed into a wall of dancing red and yellow. Every window had been blown out in the extreme heat. Twenty-foot flames roared out of them; the windows looked like horrifying mouths, stretched open and screaming in agony.

It felt good to have Dad put his arm around me, and hug me in close. We never said a word, as we stood and watched the wall of flames that had swallowed Brian's house.

If the Lutz family weren't out already, they would never be coming out.

Without a Trace

The top half of the house was all but gone now. The fire fighters had their giant hoses pointed at the smoking foundation, with pieces of wall still intact. The inside of the house was a mix of perfectly intact sections and piles of tumbled down black beams and twisted metal.

I watched and shivered as the battle weary fire fighters dragged their empty hoses back to their trucks, barely lifting their heads. They wrapped themselves in the silence of defeat. The sirens were off. It was over. They had lost.

Everyone gathered at the next door neighbour's house. Dad steered me that way to join them. Twenty or thirty people were standing around drinking coffee and asking how it could have happened and who could we call? The Lutzs were new in town, and hadn't made very many friends. Of those, no one seemed to remember having heard about any family back home.

My brain was racing and frozen stiff at the same time. Mom appeared as if by magic from out of the crowd and gave me a squeeze. When I reached around her to hug her back I checked my hands to see how badly they were shaking. My whole body felt like it was vibrating from the inside out. I might have felt shocked but shock was mixed together with fear and hope. I could feel my heart beating in my throat and all the muscles in my body twitching, and my spine was getting so tight I thought my back would snap clean in two at any minute.

The crowd was milling about me, always asking the same questions with no answers. I knew I had to talk to Mom and Dad.

It should have been easy—they were never more than an arm's length away from me.

"We have to go home," I said finally. This could not wait any longer. No matter if I was going to get into trouble or not. If there was any hope at all, I had to tell them.

They seemed to know I was serious. There was no arguing. They stood up, made their excuses and we left. We climbed silently into the car and when the doors were closed, I started talking. There was no sense waiting until we made it home. My instincts were telling me time and speed were important.

"I think I know something," I burst out. My voice was far too loud for the small car we were driving in. I cleared my throat and took a deep breath. "Look," I said, "Last week Brian noticed a repair van on his street and it stayed there for days."

Mom and Dad exchanged a quick look. Dad put the car in gear and started driving toward home.

I kept going. "Maybe it was the Witness Protection guys. Maybe they decided to move the whole family and burned down the house to cover their tracks. Brian could have been out of the house before the fire even started!"

Neither one of them was saying a word. They sat in silence and looked at one another. It felt as if they were trying to ignore my questions or were stalling. I remained quiet until we got home and sat down at the family conference center, the kitchen table.

They had had enough time to gather their thoughts so I pushed harder. "I *am* your child, and I always will be, but I'm fifteen years old! I need you to not treat me like a baby. I'm not stupid. I know what this fire could mean. Brian, his mom and dad, could be dead right now. But if there is any hope, or any chance it could be a mistake of some kind, I've got to find out. Help me! Please, what do you think," I asked. My throat was straining itself trying to sound calm.

"I'll call my police contacts and see what I can find out, okay?" Mom said after a pause. "I'm sorry Andrew, but I'm honestly not holding out too much hope. The Witness Protection Program does not, as a point of policy, burn down houses just to hide people. They move them out of the house, then sell it."

When she put it that way, my idea did sound a bit ridiculous. There had to be something we were missing. Think, think! I knew I had to think!

"Dad," I pleaded desperate to find a path out of this nightmare. "Everyone was saying how strange this house fire was. Even the firemen were saying it."

"Well," he responded in a slow voice. I could tell he was wrestling with how much he should be holding me back and how much he should be trying to help. "You have a point there. It was a strange fire. The fire marshal will have to make a report."

"You and I both know it will take weeks," I said. "We don't have weeks. Brian doesn't have weeks!"

We stared at each other, for what seemed like forever. A feeling was pacing around in the back of my head but it couldn't make its way up to the front where I could look at it. When Dad closed his eyes in a long slow blink I knew I had to push a little harder, or I would lose his help.

"You have always told me to trust my instincts. Well, my instincts tell me something about this screams that it isn't right. They also tell me I need to act fast. Now I'm asking you to put your money where your mouth is and trust my instincts too. You've had to investigate fires and natural disasters! Help me!"

After a pause, he said, "Well, let's gather up some supplies then." He slid his chair back. "The sun will be up in about an hour. We had better be there, before any one else gets there, and starts investigating."

"Thanks Dad," I said.

Dad was over by the sink putting water in the coffee maker. He stopped, pointed his organic coffee filter at me. "I'm not making any promises. I do have a few questions I would like answered myself. We're just going to have a quick look around. That's all."

Clues

Dad grabbed a small bag and filled it with flashlights, a Swiss Army knife, paint scrapers and a magnifying glass that I had seen him use to identify bugs in the woods. We headed over to what used to be Brian's house. The yellow crime scene tape was tied to stakes across the front of the yard. No policeman or fireman stood guard. In the country the firemen are all volunteers. Once the fire is out, they all go home.

The sun had not come up over the horizon and although there was enough predawn light to see without flashlights, there was not enough to peek into corners. There were no visible flames or smoke, but you could still feel the heat. The very ground was hot, wet and muddy around the house. The air smelled like wet ashes or my clothes after a weekend of camping.

There were millions of footprints pressed deeply into the soggy ground, too many to tell us anything. Dad walked straight up to the house. He looked left and right along the sections of foundation that were still standing.

Something grabbed his interest. He walked over to the side of what was once the porch and dropped down on one knee, next to the bushes that had lined the front of the porch. Dad looked over each bush and picked a few leaves. He put each leaf in the palm of his hand. I watched hopefully over his shoulder as he rubbed his hands together, to crush and heat up the different pieces. He brought his hands up to his nose. It looked like he was going to start praying with his hands pressed flat together. Instead, he made a small crack between his two thumbs and slipped his nose in to take a sniff. First, he would take a quick short sniff, then two or three long deep breaths.

I looked again and again from his face to his hands, knowing I had to be quiet for him to concentrate and desperate to know what he was trying to find out. I knew people used the smoke of different woods, or plants, to flavour foods. Hickory chips are smoldered under pork to add a hickory smoked flavour to the meat; but I was clueless as to why he was sniffing. I stood behind him hoping he would speak. "Can I help? What am I supposed to smell?" I asked, no longer able to hold it in.

"Sure. Here, smell the healthy leaf first," he said handing me the leaves he had finished crushing. "Then smell a leaf from closer to the fire. If there's something extra you can figure out what the *extra* is, and you'll know what was used to make the fire.

"Along the sides of Brian's house we'll get a hot plastic smell, because of the burnt siding. It shouldn't be there along the front of the porch, because it was painted. Different chemicals leave a smell on the things around them. Arsenic, for instance, smells like almonds."

Dad and I traveled the length of the porch crushing and sniffing, then compared notes. There was definitely a different smell on the leaves at the corner of the porch. They smelled sweeter.

"Look here Andrew. The leaves show a different curling pattern too," he said pointing at one of the bushes. "They've tried to curl away from the heat to protect themselves and keep their moisture."

It was easy to see once Dad pointed it out, that the bushes at the corners of the porch had more curled leaves than the bushes anywhere else, meaning the fire was hotter at the sides of the porch than it was along the front.

"Now these I have a problem with," Dad said tapping the black and charred corner posts sticking out from the rest of the house. "Corner posts on porches are never the *first* thing to go in a house fire. They have no reason to catch fire. They sit away from the rest of the house by several feet. There is nothing for them to catch on fire *from*."

I could feel a small lump starting in my throat and my stomach began to churn with the deep gutted hope that this was a real clue about what had happened to my friend.

Dad and I walked around the side of the house. He kept low, often dropping down on one muddy knee or the other. He swept his hand through the short grass close to the house. There were no clear footprints, but the grass had been trampled. "Andrew, how close do you think those firemen got to the house tonight?"

"I don't know, maybe twenty feet. It was too hot to get close. Why?"

"Yes, it was hot, wasn't it. So why would the firemen have done *that* during the fire?" he asked pointing at the matted down grass all along the house. Dad turned and looked me in the eye. "It's impossible to use a fire hose on a house while your feet are touching the foundation. Firemen need at least fifteen feet between them and the thing they're trying to put out. Any closer and the kickback from the hose would have planted them on their well-padded bottoms. If the firemen weren't that close to the house, who was?"

I dropped to my knees and began frantically searching through the grass hoping to find anything that would give us a clue. If only I could find a match, I could prove the fire was lit on purpose.

"Dad," I called out, "There's a swirl in the grass it shows something turned around here . . . and again over there. Without footprints I can't even guess what it was."

Dad looked at me as he was taking his Swiss Army knife out of the bag. He was rolling things around in his mind. "Staying low to the ground is the best way to avoid being seen."

It felt like something was squeezing my chest. My insides were in knots. "So you think I'm right," I asked. "Does it mean you believe me and this wasn't an accidental house fire?"

"It was a house fire Andrew. This is a house and it was definitely on fire. What this was not, was an accident. Look here." Dad pointed at a part of the wall where a few strips of siding still clung to it. He had taken his knife and scraped part of the siding.

"Something must have blown this siding off. Look at this piece here," he said pointing at the wall about two feet up, "it's been ripped. Then five feet over here is another piece that's the same. It shows us the blast spread out, it would have caught the bottom lip of each row of siding as it went up.

"All the rows below this line are still fine because the flair shape of the siding would have blown these pieces on even tighter to the house. When an airplane is flying, the pressure of the air on the wings actually presses them in tighter to the airplane's body, and helps hold them on."

He could slip a physics lesson into anything. I summed it up out loud by saying, "Fire would have melted it, not ripped it!"

"Right then," he said. "Let's see what we can find in back."

"We'd better hurry," I said. "The neighbours will be getting up any time now."

It's not very often Dad looses his cool. "They can pound sand! If anybody asks what we're doing we'll tell them you're working on your fire safety badge for Boy Scouts," he growled.

At the back of the house, Dad inched along the foundation. He seemed more interested in the grass than before. Several times he picked up pieces of soil and rubbed them between his fingers, then smelled them, cleaning his hands off before each new sniff. He was running out of clean places to wipe his hands. Our knees were wet and caked in mud. Dad's shirt and pants were covered in soot, ashes and dirt. The air smelled sharp and stung my nose. I knew our clothes smelled the same.

I started following a similar pattern in the siding. It led me to back door. I was a little surprised by what I saw, so I took one step away from the house to get a better look. The back door was the most intact thing on the entire house. The glass was gone but the door and the walls around it were unmarked by flames.

I turned away from the house and headed over to where my father crouched in the grass, sweeping his hand back and forth. My foot thumped into something hard. I bent over to pick up what looked like a big piece of glass.

"Dad!" I called out holding the glass out in front of me. "I think I found something!"

Dad popped up and jogged over. He took the glass disc out of my hand and flipped it over a few times. His eyes shifted. He gazed back to the door.

Finally, he made a fist and held it up directly in front of his face. He took the piece of glass, balanced it on top of his fist and stared at it. The piece of glass was bigger than his fist. After a full minute, he lowered the piece of glass just enough so we could lock eyes over top of the glass disc.

"Fires don't make perfect circle holes in glass doors," he said. "Especially ones that are just big enough for someone to reach their hands in to undo a lock. We know whoever set the fire went inside the house."

"Why go in a house you plan on burning down?" I asked.

"Exactly," he said, dropping the piece of glass back to the lawn where I had found it.

"What are you doing? We need that! It's important!"

"It's evidence, son. Even if we have tampered with it a little, we still can't take it away from a crime scene. Besides it's already told us all it can. Come on, let's see what else we can find. They had to get here, and leave here, somehow. The driveway would have been a little too obvious. Maybe we can figure out how they did get here. It might tell us something."

We spaced ourselves about five feet apart and started walking in a zigzag pattern further and further away from the house. It took a few passes before anything started to stand out. Eventually the matted down grass started to give way to large clusters of footprints. After a few more passes those footprints became fewer and fewer. Finally the thing we were searching for appeared: a cluster of five or six sets of footprints — one set coming from across the field and the other set returning.

"How far apart would you say those footprints are?" Dad asked, pointing at one of the sets with its toes pointed toward the house.

I knelt down in the grass and fanned my hand out between two of the prints. Excitement and hope had been rising in me, like the pressure in a volcano, as we crossed the field. The grass wasn't wet from the firemen's hose but it was damp from early morning dew. The damp grass on my palm released the trigger and I shuddered. "Eighteen inches apart I'd say."

"What does that tell you?"

"They were taking shorter, cautious steps."

"Right. What about these ones?" he asked pointing at the set of prints going the other direction.

I moved over to where he was and crouched down by the second set. "Almost a three foot stride here." I looked up at Dad's grim face. "A running stride! They were running away!"

"Exactly," he confirmed, reaching out a hand to help me up. Then pointing toward the edge of the field, "The tracks divide into two groups right up here and both sets end at the edge of the highway. There were at least two vehicles."

There was no sense looking any further. It was time to go home and tell Mom.

Awake

The first of Brian's senses to come back was his hearing. He heard their voices before his eyes could see anything but black. He had woken up in a moving vehicle. He could tell by the radio and the rumble of the tires on the pavement.

He forced himself to blink and his vision slowly cleared. He could see he was in the back of a cargo van. There were no seats, other than the driver's and one for a passenger. The high headrests of the seats made it impossible to see who was driving. Only a black sleeve was visible on the middle armrest of each seat.

Making sure he did not move his head, or any part of his body, Brian shifted his eyes to try to look around. He was lying on his side on the floor, with his hands tied behind his back. The ropes were tight but not biting into his skin. The floor was bare metal and more than a little cold.

Brian had been placed with his back next to the wall. He looked toward the rear of the van and saw one person dressed in black. He sat against the side door across from Brian, but Brian couldn't see his face. There was something in the man's hands and all his attention was focused on it.

Near the man in black, Brian saw his mother. Her long hair had fallen over her face so he couldn't see if she was awake. She was wearing a nightgown with small pink flowers on it. Her arms were stretched behind her back in an uncomfortable looking position. He knew her hands must also be tied.

Brian closed his eyes once more and tried to think. Where was his father? Where were they headed? His brain was slowly coming up to speed. A sudden thought burst into his head. THE BAG! Where was the backpack?

Brian took a small breath and shrugged his shoulders. He was careful not to move too much, not wanting to attract the attention of the fellow across from him. A wave of heat and relief swept over him as he realized he could still feel the pressure of the backpack's straps.

His senses began to go fuzzy again. Brian didn't fight it as he pressed his back into the bag. There was hope, he thought, as he drifted back into an unnatural sleep. With the backpack properly fastened, it was quicker for the figures in black to take Brian the way he was and not waste time taking the bag off.

The next time he woke up it was, again, his hearing that came back first. He could hear a bird very far away. There was no sound from an engine and no radio. There was no road noise either. He was no longer in the van

As before, he was lying on his side — the other side this time. He could feel his right shoulder pressing into something soft beneath him. His mind was fully awake now, but he kept his eyes closed and commanded his body to stay still.

He opened his eyes, and saw his mom lying on a cot directly across the room from him. She lay flat on her stomach, with her hands tied together resting on the small of her back. She had her face turned toward him, but her eyes were still closed.

There did not seem to be anyone else in the room. Moving his head off the pillow, Brian could see he was lying on a cot much like his mom's. There was only one other piece of furniture in the room: a small metal chair sitting against the wall between the two beds.

The smooth and varnished surface of the almond coloured logs told Brian, very clearly, they were in a fancy and expensive log cabin. The floor had been done in thin, glossy, hardwood boards. The light shade in the middle of the ceiling was made of stained glass.

'Think,' Brian told himself. Mentally, he went through all the things that he had stuffed into his backpack.

Yesterday when he had left Andrew's house, Brian had had only enough time to go home and put the two motion detector alarms up — one in the front hall way, the other at the back door — before his mom had come in. He hadn't been able to sneak outside to put the tracking transmitter on his dad's car.

The tracking transmitter was still in the bag, and they had put a voice transmitter disguised as a baseball cap in the bag, too. Brian felt sure he would still have that. The alarm pen looked like a regular pen. You could even write with it. If the kidnappers happened to try the button that turned on the transmitter, it wouldn't do anything. The only way they could tell it was a transmitter would be to open the pen up or have a receiver in hand and set on the right frequency, or station.

It was like a radio. If a radio was not set on the right frequency, you couldn't hear the music. The radio station could play the best music in the world, and transmit full blast, but if you weren't tuned in to the same station, you'd never know it existed.

For the next hour Brian stared at his sleeping mother and tried to make a plan. There were so many pieces of the puzzle that were missing. Would Andrew, or anyone, even be looking for them? How long would it take for the firemen or police to realize his family hadn't been left in the house? What transmitter should he use first?

Brian realized none of this would matter if he couldn't turn any of the transmitters on. With his hands tied behind his back there was no way he could even get at them. The only way would be for whoever it was that tied him, to come and untied him. It didn't seem likely. If they were going to untie him they would have done it by now.

The epiphany came to Brian as he remembered a movie about an escape artist named Harry Houdini. He could wiggle out of straight jackets and chains with locks because he was so flexible. It didn't hurt either when his wife had slipped him the key as she kissed him for good luck. Brian wondered how tightly his hands had been tied.

While testing the straps around his wrists, Brian had to shift his weight off his shoulder. The cot creaked in protest at the movement. His blood raced with fear, but he forced himself to close his eyes and lie perfectly still, pleading silently with the cot for it to not squeak again. He listened to see if the noise had alerted anyone to the fact he was awake.

During the next few minutes his ears strained to hear anything other than his own pulse, now roaring in his ears. Perhaps he and his mother were on the second floor, and movement they made would not be heard from downstairs. Brian decided it was time to test his idea.

He rolled forward slightly to free his arm from under his side. With most of his weight on his knee and his shoulder, Brian pushed his hands past his hips and over his bottom. With a deep breath, he was able to slide the strap halfway down his thighs. Slowly he rolled onto his back. If he curled his chin down to his chest it gave him just enough reach to stretch his arms and slip the strap over his heels and past his toes. His brought his hands up in front of his face and stared at the black Velcro straps around his wrists. He willed them not to be real, simply to vanish.

The movement didn't use a lot of muscle, but with every nerve in his body firing and twitching, it forced a cold sweat all over his skin. The fine hairs that covered his arms and the back of his neck were standing straight up. He used his thumbs and pointer fingers to undo the two buckles across his chest. He reached up over his head to grab the handle at the top of the backpack and tipping his head to the side, pulled the bag over his head. The bag landed square in his lap. Brian said a silent prayer as he undid the zipper of his bag. His prayers were answered. Everything was still inside.

Taking a deep calming breath, Brian glanced toward the window. Outside was bright but cloudy. He had no idea how long ago they had been taken: one day, two, maybe three? He didn't know what time it was now. His watch was still on the bedside table at home.

Okay, he said to himself. *When I didn't turn up at school, Andrew probably would have called me after he got home. If he checked the alarms, he would have seen that someone had tripped the motion detector. Maybe he figured it out right away and is looking for me.*

What would he look for first?

The first thing he pulled out of the bag was the alarm transmitter. He set it in his lap and stared at it disappointedly. The alarm transmitter wouldn't do any good if he was more than five miles away, and the battery would only last about six hours. Brian shrugged. What were the chances of Andrew looking for them already? He put it back in the bag.

He then pulled out the baseball cap with the voice transmitter hidden inside it. He turned it over in his hand a few times, studying it. The signal in this guy wasn't very strong, and would only reach about half as far as the alarm. The upside was, if he was close enough, he could tell Andrew exactly where his family was.

The downside was he couldn't tell them *where they were,* because he didn't know! Brian looked around the room scanning every inch of the walls in hopes of finding any clues. The log cabin had electricity, so they couldn't be too far into the woods.

The heaviest thing in the bag was the tracking transmitter. This would tell Andrew exactly where they were! *Okay, think clearly,* he told himself. He had to get this right! The tracking transmitter had a GPS head in it, and could transmit their exact coordinates to Andrew and show him were they were! Distance wouldn't matter, because it has a built in cellphone that could call back to Andrew's computer!

Brian decided to turn on the tracking transmitter. Using his shaking fingers he unscrewed the lid and opened the black metal box. Inside was a simple on/off switch; everything else had to be programmed via a serial port from a computer. He and Andrew had programmed the transmitter to have the motion detector turned on so the transmitter would sleep, sort of, while his dad's car was parked at work all day or in the driveway all night. When the car did start moving it would turn on automatically and tell them where the car went.

Once the switch was turned on and the lid tightened again Brian placed it, too, into the bag. It felt good to know he was doing *something* to help save them. The transmitter wouldn't work until he started moving around, but it would at least be ready.

Brian looked over at his mother. She still hadn't moved. The need to do something more surged through him. He reached back into the bag and took out the alarm transmitter. Chewing nervously on his bottom lip, he took a deep breath to steel himself to the decision he was about to make. He pushed the red button on the ball point pen and put it carefully back in the bag.

He was set. Brian started doing everything in reverse, to get the bag back on properly. In no time at all, it was once again on his back, with the bag zipped closed and the Velcro straps in place.

With everything in place, Brian lay back down on his side. He was breathing heavily and his arms were shaking. The excitement had make his head hurt but still his mind raced. Maybe this place has bad cellphone reception? The GPS head would have a hard time seeing the satellites from inside the house. It could work, but it would work better if he got closer to a window.

The Jigsaw Puzzle

Mom met Dad and me at the door. "Found something did you?" Mom said, looking right into Dad's eyes. When he nodded, she hurried us in. "Let's share notes, I've found a few things of my own. I made breakfast while I was waiting for you to get back. We can talk and eat at the same time. You first. What did you find?"

Dad and I took turns telling her, and Mom told us about her call to some of her contacts at the Agency. None of them had heard of any plans to move the Lutz family.

The local police department had received an alarm signal from the Lutz house, at about midnight. It had stopped one minute later. The fire would have shorted out the battery fairly quickly. They thought it was a false alarm. When the police called the Lutz's house to make sure everything was all right, there was no answer. It was standard routine to send over a car, so they did.

"You two found enough to prove the house was set on fire, on purpose," said Mom.

"I know they got out," I said. "I just know it. Why would someone bother to go into the house if they were only going to burn it down anyway? Unless it was to get the people, or something, out."

Dad leaned back in his chair with his arms crossed over his chest, and a dark scowl. "Whoever started the fire should get a substantial raise. They knew what they were doing and they were good at it."

"Exactly," said Mom. "From what you two say, somebody wanted to make a big show with this house fire, but why? I really should have wired their house when they first moved in."

"The transmitters," I whispered.

"What transmitters?" she called after me, but I did not stop to answer.

By the time they reached me, I was already checking for new files. The tracking transmitter hadn't been turned on yet. There was nothing there. Next I checked the alarm file. *BINGO*!! I screamed, "*I've got something*!!"

Mom turned her attention from the computer screen to me. "What are you trying to tell us here? How did you get into my software?"

"Mom, I've been playing with your software my entire life," I said. "You've made me run whole programs for you while you were out there scaring the neighbours."

"You're not in trouble here," she said moving close to me. She put her hands on my shoulders and looked me hard in the eyes. "This is the time for you to be completely honest with me. NO secrets! What else is going on I don't know about?"

I explained. "Brian and I have been fooling around with some of your spy gear after school. He was worried because of the cable van, so we decided to wire his place and see if there was anything suspicious going on."

Pushing me out of the chair, Mom moved in front of the computer and started striking keys. "What have you got?" she asked.

"Something from the motion detector we put inside their house," I said, pointing at the screen. "I haven't pulled the file yet but there is something there. I didn't go home with him so he must have gotten it set up last night before his parents got home."

"What else?" she asked sharply, clicking away at the keyboard.

I listed off what we had taken, how and where we planned to set each alarm up. I reached over her shoulders and pointed at the information now on the screen. "Look, both alarms were tripped."

"The first alarm," I explained, "was for the hallway by the back door. The program shows it detected something moving for a full five seconds. The second alarm, in the hall, saw something for eight seconds. The two times overlap. No one can be in two places at once, so there was more than one person in there. Dad and I figured on five or six. Maybe they all entered the house."

"Be careful you don't jump to conclusions," Mom warned. "But I do agree it seems likely there were at least two different people in the house."

"I think Andrew is right," Dad said.

"Okay," said Mom, pointing at the second screen as is came up. "Now we have something. Look, four different alarms, one big alarm going in and three alarms coming out. Each of the exiting alarms takes ten to fifteen seconds. If I read these alarms right, it took them longer to leave the house than it took for them to go in." She spun in her seat to look at us. "I'm safe in saying more people left the house, than went in."

Dad put his hand on my shoulder. I turned to look up at him. "Andrew your friend and his parents are alive. Those people wouldn't have taken them out of the house if they were going to kill them."

Captured

Brian woke up at the low and urgent sound of his mother's voice. "Brian," she whispered, "please baby, open your eyes!" The fear in her voice caused a knife-like pain in the middle of Brian's chest. He knew if they were going to get out of this alive, it was going to be up to him. He had the backpack and it held their only hope.

Her face was as white as if she was sick. The flowered nightgown made her appear even sicker. For the first time in his memory, she looked . . . very small. Her bottom lip trembled into a smile, as she realized his eyes were open and looking at her.

"I guess you caught me napping," Brian said trying to maintain a normal voice.

His mother flinched and her eyes shot toward the door.

"It's all right, Mom," Brian continued. "There's no one who can hear us. I haven't heard a sound from downstairs. If we can't hear them, they can't hear us."

"Are you all right?" she asked.

"I'm fine, Mom," he said, trying to reassure her a little.

"Have you seen your father," she asked. "Do you know where he is?"

"No," he said. He saw the worry in her eyes. "Just because he's not in our room, doesn't mean he's not in this house. They could be keeping us separated for now."

They were quiet again for a long time. Brian watched tears escaped his mother's tightly closed eyes. They ran down the side of her nose and dropped onto the mattress. She bit down on her lips and took a deep breath through her nose, fighting for control.

Brain tried to decide how much to tell her about the transmitters in his backpack. In the end he felt it was better to give her the same hope he had. "Mom," he finally said, "I have to tell you something."

He started at the beginning and told her all about the first night when he had slept over at Andrew's house. How they had fooled around with some of the electronic spy gear Andrew's mom kept for testing. He told her all about the tracking games they had played and the different transmitters they had tried.

She said nothing, but listened with her eyebrows raised in half question, and disbelief. He told her about the part when he woke up to the sound of feet running in the hallway. She smiled proudly, when he told her about jumping out of bed to put his knapsack on, and buckling it into place.

"I've already turned on the alarm transmitter but it's only good for about six hours. I can't tell how long I've been asleep. Or how long I've been awake for that matter! So I'm not sure if it's still transmitting or not. I don't want to turn everything on at once because when the batteries run out we won't have anything."

"You said you had a cellphone?" Brian's mom asked.

"Well yeah . . . I suppose . . . " Brian answered slowly. "It's part of the tracking transmitter."

"Why don't you call them on the cellphone?" she asked, in a surprised voice. "Tell them we've been kidnapped? Tell them we're being held captive in a cabin. Maybe they can start searching and eventually find us?"

"It's not that kind of cellphone, Mom," Brian explained. "It's just the guts of the cellphone, stuffed inside a big black thing, like a metal brick. You program it by connecting it to a computer before you use it. Even if I could get inside it, there are no keypads or numbers I could dial with."

"Wait a minute," she said. "You told me you already turned on the alarm and the tracking transmitter thing, right?"

"Yeah," Brian answered. "But I don't know how long ago."

Lifting her head from the mattress for the first time, she asked, "*How* did you turn anything on, with your hands tied behind your back?"

A big smile spread across Brian's face. "You watch," he said as he shifted his weight once more onto his shoulder and repeated his Houdini trick. He didn't pull the backpack all the way over his head though. He lifted it by the handle for her to see.

He went through the reverse actions to get his hands in place behind his back. He warned his mother he didn't want their kidnappers knowing he could do this. The trick might come in handy later.

They tried to make conversation every once in a while, but there was nothing really to say. Brian and his mother looked at one another in silence or stared at the door. The same door the kidnappers would be coming through, sooner or later. The only question was, when?

They were both hungry and felt sore from sitting and lying for so long. It was starting to get dark when they heard a noise, more like the memory of a noise, than an actual noise itself. Within a few minutes the sound began to take shape, the way bells would if you rang them under water.

He knew from the steady thump, thump that someone was climbing a set of stairs. As he had feared, the sound stopped in front of their bedroom door. There was no clatter of keys, only the hollow echo of a single deadbolt sliding open. A slow, heavy steel clunk that left no question in anybody's mind about the size of the bolt holding them in the room.

Brian had not taken his eyes off the door. The man who entered the room looked like a WWF Wrestler. Brian couldn't help but wonder how he had managed to make it through the door. His shoulders must have been three feet wide and two feet thick.

"I've brought you something to eat." His deep voice filled the room and made the walls shake. He wasn't yelling. His voice simply fit his body. Three hundred pounds of bench press muscles, a shaved head and a square jaw. He was dressed in black except for his forearms, which were covered with angry looking tattoos.

"It's bacon and eggs," he said, once more in his deep hollow voice. "I cooked it myself, so I hope you like it." Then as an after thought he added, "If not, just lie."

"Wait," called Brian's mother, leaning forward on her cot. "Where is my husband? How long are you going to be keeping us here?"

The giant answered, "Your husband is downstairs. We're going to be here for a while. The boss thought if you were all together, you might get some stupid ideas. Keith is staying in a different room. He is all right for now. We're not your problem, we're only a delivery service."

While he was talking, he placed the plates of food he had been carrying on their beds. He reached behind Brian's mom first and undid the Velcro strap, which held her hands together. He waited for her to rub her wrists and handed her a plate.

Brian was a little afraid when the man moved toward him. He knew it was impossible for his captor to tell he had slipped his hands around in front of him earlier, but still he held his breath as the man reached behind him.

The man continued to talk as he went back to the door and turned on the light. "The plan is to stay here for about six days. We need to wait until the locals stop looking for you . . . that is if they are looking for you at all. We have five days left."

"Then what?" Brian's mother blurted out.

She hadn't touched her food yet though Brian knew she must be as hungry as he. She had focused her attention on getting information. Brian listened as well.

"Then we take you back to Chicago. They can decide what to do with you there," the large man said, closing the door behind him as he left.

After about an hour he returned. He took away the empty plates and glasses. Brian and his mother were allowed to go to the bathroom — Brian's mother went first. By the time Brian returned to the bedroom, his mother already had her hands fastened with Velcro, once more, behind her back.

Seeing him approach, Brian instinctively reached up to double-check the clasps on his backpack. "What is the matter kid. Are you afraid I will steal your books?" the man grumbled.

"No", Brian replied. "I always carry it and besides, I have a lot of homework to do. I don't want to forget it."

The giant laughed, "I don't think you have to worry about homework where you're going."

Call in the Big Guns

ours later, the signal sounded like a travel alarm clock going off in the basement. I didn't know what it was, but Mom did. She jumped out of the kitchen chair so high I half expected to see a small terrier hanging off her bottom, ran past me and took the stairs to the basement two at a time.

"We got something!!" she screamed. "Come on baby! Come on, come on, come on! Andrew," she called up the steps, "What are your intervals?"

I was already halfway across the kitchen, running toward the stairs. "Five minutes, I think. What have we got? Is he alive?"

"I'll let you know for sure in about four and a half minutes," she answered.

Dad was also on the move from the living room and coming fast. The thumping of his feet on the hardwood floor matched my heart, pounding inside my chest.

In the office we stared at a simple, black metal box — more specifically, at the center of the box, where a small blue circle glowed up at us like the face on a wristwatch. Printed on the face of the watch were the letters N, E, S and W. They were positioned where the 12, 3, 6 and 9 should have been.

If the signal were strong enough, the box would be able to tell us what direction it had come from. A small black arrow would point at "N" for north, or "NW" for northwest and so on. If it wasn't strong enough, or was too far away, the box wouldn't be able to give the direction. It would only flash a small light and make another travel alarm clock sound, to let you know a signal was picked up.

The three yells came so close together, it sounded like one voice. Dad, Mom and I were all screaming and grabbing each other. The alarm had sounded again.

"Bless your little soul, Brian!" Mom cried.

"There's no direction," I said in disbelief. "He's trying to tell us where he is but the signal isn't strong enough!"

"Quick," Mom said, picking up the small black box. "Get in the car. We have to drive to the top of a hill, so we can pick up a better signal."

"No," I said, grabbing the black box out of her hands, and heading up the stairs. "We don't have time for that. The alarm is only good for a few hours." I had a better idea. Tucking the box into the back of my pants I made for the back yard.

Every kid has dreamed about getting on the roof of the house. I was the one kid on the planet whose parents *sent* them there. Dad and I would go up there to look at star constellations, or watch meteor showers. Mom would send me to the roof so I could adjust antennas.

To me it was part of a routine. I put the picnic table against the side of the shed and climbed onto the roof, took out the box and waited for another signal.

Nothing.

Not high enough and I knew it. Grabbing the top of a piece of plywood Dad had leaned up against the far side of the shed, I heaved with all my might. Suddenly, it began to move, throwing me off balance. When I looked down I could see Dad standing on the ground. He was picking up the other end of the plywood and shoving it up toward me.

I slid the plywood across the roof of the shed toward the garage. It was like a giant set of steps, going from the shed to the garage and the garage to the main part of the house. The plywood met with the garage wall and started to slide down on the far end, coming to rest on the top of the window ledge. It sagged as I started across, but it held.

Reaching the garage, I grabbed the rain gutter and pulled myself up. From there, it was a steep climb to the top of the house. The shingles were rough but my sneakers gripped them without any real problem.

In moments I had reached the peak of the roof. I pulled out the black box. Standing as tall as I could, I held it over my head until I thought my arms would break. If either of my parents had been calling after me to be careful I didn't hear them. Everything in my body told me to reach for the stars.

(Beep)

I bent my knees a little, so I wouldn't fall over. Pulling the box down to eye level, I could see the screen I yelled, "North! He's north of here!"

"Stay where you are Andrew," Mom called up. "You need to get three or four more signals, to make sure you have the right direction. I'm going to go make a phone call. Be careful!"

"Remember, if you fall off the roof and break both your legs, don't come running to me," Dad said once Mom had gone inside the house.

We smiled at each other. Both of us were remembering Mom had jokingly said that very thing before sending me up on the roof the first time, when I was only seven years old.

The next three signals were from the north, so now we had something to work with. I climbed down and went back in the house to find Mom. She was dashing around the kitchen making a pot of coffee and chopping fruit and veggies for a snack.

"It's been a whole day," I said, moving to get out of the way and sit at the table. "Why would he wait a whole day before sending me something?"

"I don't know, Andrew," answered my mom, still chopping. "Someone from NAIPA should be here soon. I called one of my contacts there and told them we had reason to believe the family is still alive. They're sending an agent to see what we have."

"I hope whoever they send is better than the last guy. What kind of protection did he give them? That guy should be fired!"

Mom looked at me with surprise. "Good point" she said. Then chopping a little more slowly, she added, "Maybe you had better let me do the talking."

"Why," I asked. "I know more about what Brian can do than you could ever guess."

"True," she said. "But please, just go along with whatever I say. Okay?"

I didn't answer her. There wasn't any point. She was off in her own world. She stared off into space not noticing that she was spreading peanut butter onto the carrot sticks. The only thing left was the eyebrow pulling.

I returned to the roof to make sure there was no change in the direction of the alarm. If the direction changed it would mean Brian and his family were moving. Not moving was better. It was easier to hit a target when it is stationary.

From my perch I watched as people arrived. By the time I came down and went back inside, everyone was talking, drinking and snacking all at the same time. Mom's peanut-buttered carrots were still piled high on the tray but the rest of the vegetable tray had been eaten.

Mom was talking to a group of people I had never seen. In fact, the only person outside of my family I did know was Don Proctor, that slimy black snake guy in spandex — this time he was in a grey suit. Everyone was talking about how tomorrow they'd start searching the northern part of town, going door to door, then spread out like a fan from the town limits.

They hoped they would narrow down where Brian's family was before sunset. Then they'd call in the FBI. It was their job to do all the sneaking around corners, crashing into houses and gunfire stuff. The NAIPA guys stayed well out of it.

"Excuse me," I said loud enough to get everyone's attention. Mom was shaking her head and giving me a stern look. "You people keep talking like we aren't going to do anything until tomorrow.

We don't have that much time. We should be out there now when we at least know where we're going."

Mom had crossed the room and was trying to turn me toward the stairs. "Andrew, I know how upset you must be. We should go downstairs and talk for a few minutes," she said in a loud voice, which wasn't meant for me.

She turned to the crowd in our kitchen. "You will have to excuse us for a minute." I let her lead me downstairs into the office. Everything had been put away. It looked like a picture out of a catalogue. There was nothing on her usually cluttered desk, no wires tacked up on the walls, no antennas or equipment at all. It was spotless.

"What in the world happened in here?" I teased, trying to break some of the mounting tension.

Mom looked me in the eyes. "These people don't need to know what I do, thank you very much. Those fellows up there are regular force policemen. They aren't with NAIPA or the FBI. There's more to it than what you think. I'm not the one in control here. I don't call the shots."

I took a deep breath. "So what they were saying is true. They have no plans to do anything, or even starting looking, until tomorrow?"

"That's right. The FBI is sending an agent to deal with this but he can't get here before tomorrow sometime."

"We could be losing the signal by then," I told her.

"Yes," she said, "but I have to tell you something. I told them Brian's dad had told me he had a quartz chip implanted in his body and I happened to remember the frequency. So yesterday, while I was goofing around in the basement, I tried that same frequency. Surprisingly, some of my bird tracking equipment picked it up and it wasn't coming from the same direction as his house; so he wasn't in the house fire, like we first thought. Crystals don't run out of batteries so they think we have all the time in the world and we do; as long as Andrew and his family aren't moving, we're pretty safe in not rushing crazily into this thing. Let the people who know how to handle this kind of situation do their job."

I asked, "What about the snake guy who came over earlier. He knows what you do?"

"Not really. Mr. Proctor knows I have security clearance and a scramble phone. But that's it."

"So we're not doing anything to find Brian until tomorrow," I repeated to be certain.

"Right, "she said. "People don't just run off and do something without a plan, Andrew. Especially the people we're really waiting for. It is their job to find your friend and bring him home. We have to wait and see what they do."

I couldn't believe what she was telling me.

"What about the other stuff," I asked. "Aren't you even going to tell them Brian might be able to use a voice transmitter, or the GPS tracking system?"

"NO", she answered in a stern voice. "When NAIPA and the FBI get here, fine, but there's no reason for the local police departments to know about it yet. We haven't had a signal from either of those transmitters. There's no point in the people upstairs knowing they even exist."

We stared at each other for a few seconds, then I nodded my head. I knew there was no arguing with her. Mom put her hand on my shoulder as she walked past me. I was alone in the office. Just where I knew I needed to be.

I waited for a few seconds after she went back upstairs. Then I started hunting through the drawers and closets. Where would Mom hide her equipment if she was in a hurry? I asked myself.

I ran to the laundry room and picked up the lid to the big basket. It normally hid stinky clothes. I pulled off a sweatshirt off the top of the pile and there was a bundle of antenna wires. *Bingo!*

Digging deeper, I found more of the things she had decided to put out of sight. I wouldn't be able to carry her computer or the laptop and ride my bike at the same time. Without me having a car, the part of the vehicle tracking system Brian had didn't do me much good; but the alarm was going and I knew how to track that.

I grabbed a pair of earphones and a receiver that matched the one I had been holding on the roof. This one, about the size of a Walkman could also pick up signals for the voice transmitter, so I could pick up the signal from whichever transmitter Brian had. All I had to do was set the receiver to the right frequency. If it picked up Brian's voice, I would be able to hear it through the earphones. I put the sweatshirt back in the hamper and headed upstairs.

No one seemed to notice when I entered the kitchen and grabbed a bottle of water from the fridge. They didn't notice when I left the house either. I called over my shoulder; "I'm going back up on the roof."

I didn't go to the roof. I went to the garage and grabbed my bike. Packing the receiver, my bottle of water, my wallet and a sweatshirt into my backpack, I set out on my own. The wires for the earphones made it look like I was listening to a CD. I started biking north, aiming for the mountains. It was a huge area to search but I was not going to wait one more minute.

It seemed impossible that a few days ago Brian and I had been goofing around with this exact same receiver. He had spent a lot of time at our house helping me sneak Mom's equipment out and playing with it. We'd tracked each other on our bikes. Took turns putting a transmitter in our backpack. After a ten-minute head start, the other person would see how quickly they could find the first. Now I was using it for real.

On The Move

When the giant came back to turn the lights out for the night, he seemed tense, unlike the last time when he had been relaxed and calm. Now his lips were pressed together into a firm, straight line. He was rougher, but not unkind, when he undid Brian's hands and told him to go to the bathroom.

Brian guessed this must be the last pee before bed. He felt like a puppy. While he was in the bathroom, Brian overheard the man telling his mother that Keith was fine and that he had not had supper but was sleeping quietly. Brian didn't believe it for a minute. Mob guys never let you sleep peacefully, he thought. They might hang you upside down by your toes for the night, at least according to Hollywood movies, but they never let you sleep peacefully.

When Brian was once again sitting on his bed with his hands strapped together behind his back, he heard, "Sleep tight young fellow. We have a long ride ahead of us tomorrow."

Brian's ears perked to attention. "What do you mean tomorrow," he asked. "I thought we were staying here for another five days? I was starting to like your cooking."

"Change of plans," the big man boomed, not picking up on the joke. "We are heading to Chicago at first light. We should be there by Monday. It is a long drive, so try and get some rest."

Brian's mind was racing but he couldn't think of a single question. At least, not one he might get an honest answer to.

"Good night folks," the man said as he shut out the light and left the room. The sudden darkness made the bolt sliding into place sound like a cannon.

Brian looked toward his mother. "Something must have happened if they've changed their plans like this."

"Brian," she said desperately, "We can't go back to Chicago! I have no idea what they're going to do to us there, or why we have to go all that way for them to do it. But we can't ever allow ourselves, or your father, to go back there."

Brian's eyes had adjusted to the darkness. The moon was almost full and shining right in the window. He started to wiggle around on the bed. This time it was easier to slip his arms around his bottom and past his feet.

With his hands now in front of him, Brian started using his teeth to grab at the end of the Velcro strap. After three or four tries the strap lifted with a ripping sound.

His mother whispered urgently, "What're you doing? How are you going to fasten that up again? You know they're going to come back!"

"Of course I know," he answered. "I've got to get a signal out."

Brian tested the floor with his foot to see if it would squeak when he stood on it, but it didn't. Feeling confident, he got up and moved quickly toward the window. Without saying a word, his mother shifted her weight over her feet and followed him to the window, her hands still strapped behind her back.

She waited in silence as he first looked the window over to see if there were any wires, little red lights from lazer beams, or electrical tape. He knew from Andrew these could be used as part of an alarm system and the people downstairs might have tried to set one up. There was nothing he could see, so he tested the lock.

The lock was a simple slide bolt but someone had snapped the handle off. There was nothing to pull the lock out of the hole. Brian went to his bag and grabbed his library card. His hands were shaking as slipped the card in past the end of the bolt, hoping he could force it out of the locked position.

The bold wouldn't slide. The whole lock had to come off.

He grabbed his pencil case and dumped everything out on the bed. He found the plastic triangle that lives in the pencil case of every student in the free world. The one that gets shoved around and waits for the one week in your whole life you use it in grade ten geometry.

He tipped the plastic triangle up at an odd angle and worked the point into the head of a screw. His first try made the plastic twist. Desperate, Brian tried again. Slowly he increased the amount of strength he used, until he thought the plastic would snap.

The screw let go its grip with a quick, half turn. Brian let out the breath he didn't even know he was holding. Eventually the screw had come up high enough that he could grab it with his fingers. He stashed it near the corner of the window.

By the time the fourth screw came out, two corners had broken off the triangle and Brian's head was wet with sweat. He picked up the entire slide bolt and moved it aside to join his collection of screws. The window slid open easily and without a sound.

"What are you planning?" Brian's mother asked in a shaky voice. She had been silent the entire time he had worked at the screws.

"They're leaving us alone," he told her. "He said we're leaving at dawn, so we have at least four or five hours to ourselves. I think we could get away but I'm not going without Dad. The alarm transmitter will be dead in a few hours. I'm going to the highest place I can find. The signal will travel further. Cellphone coverage is a little hit and miss when you get out in the woods. The more I move around out there the better our chances of hitting a place where the tracking transmitter can send out our location and tell Andrew where we are. Other than that . . . I guess I'll put on the voice transmitter and scream 'mayday'.

"We don't even know if anyone is looking for us. We're running out of time. We have until dawn. Maybe someone will pick me up on a CB radio. I don't know, but we have to do something."

"Which one of us is supposed to be the parent here?" his mother asked, wistfully. "I'm so proud of you and so scared at the same time. I know I should be going and not you but you know what you are doing and I don't. How you know all this is beyond me!"

By this time Brian had put his backpack into place and climbed up into the window frame. Turning toward his mother he smiled. "My friend taught me everything I know, Mom. You really should be more careful who you let me hang with." He winked at her. "I think he may be a bad influence."

They looked at each other quickly and a silent agreement was made. Brian turned. It was his first look at their surroundings. Trees. He could see plenty of peaks or rises in the land and they were all covered in trees. First he had to try to figure out a way down the two stories to the ground directly beneath him. To the left was nothing but a long, flat wall. About eight feet over was a second window, but Brian couldn't see how it was going to help him.

To the right there was a porch. It had a sloped roof, which started about five feet away. Brian looked up at the eavestrough. It ran the full length of the main roof above him. Grabbing the window frame and pivoting, Brian stood up and stretched up to test the eavestrough, which proved strong enough to hold his weight. Leaning as far as he could toward the porch, he grabbed the eavestrough with his hands, and swung free of the window.

He waited until he stopped swinging and used his hands to inch toward the porch roof. His arms began to burn with the effort. If only he had known all those flexed arm hangs in gym class were actually going to help him one day, he might have even tried to stay up for the full five minutes, he thought.

The porch roof banged his knee as he climbed on it. Keeping as quiet as possible, he turned and slid down the roof. It was cold and his toes were tingling. When he reached the edge he jumped easily to the ground where he stayed perfectly still for a full minute, listening for sounds from inside the cabin.

Without looking back, even to wave to his mother, he started running. He could see where he was going in the moonlight. From the window he had seen a hill. It wasn't the highest one around but with only a few hours to run there, send a message and run back, it would have to do.

After twenty minutes Brian's bare feet were sore. Luckily the ground was mostly mossy. If it hadn't been, he doubted he would have even made it this far. He was breathing hard, sucking air into his lungs in great gulps. He was on a rise in the land and couldn't catch his breath; it seemed the perfect time to stop running and turn on the voice transmitter.

Dropping to one knee and reaching into the bag, he pulled out the ball cap. He turned on the hidden voice transmitter by twisting the small button at the very top of the cap, then jammed the hat onto his head. The beak of the hat blocked out too much moonlight and made it harder to see, so he turned it around backward, like one of the cool kids at the mall.

"Hello," he called out into space. "Can anyone hear me? My family and I have been kidnapped by the mob and are being held in a hideout in the mountains . . . ra-ha-ha." Brian burst into laughter. It sounded so silly when he said it out loud. He tried again, "Help! Help! This isn't a joke! Please!"

He kept talking and yelling, as he reached into his bag once more. Taking out what looked like a large black brick, Brian held it high over his head and shook it. He knew the motion detector would have turned it on by now, but he wasn't going to take any chances.

Keeping the hat on his head and putting the brick back in the bag, Brian stood once more, and headed off again. He ran. He jogged. He called for help. Finally he came to the top of a small rise.

There was nowhere else to run, so he sat down on the cold ground and started talking. "My name is Brian Lutz and if anyone can hear this, please call the police and let them know you heard this. We're being held in a log cabin with stained glass light shades and a big porch. It's on the side of a hill and has a dirt driveway.

If you could, please call the Johnstons at 555-9116. Tell them you heard this message. They would be very happy to get this call. Tell them that my family and I are in the mountains and really, really need help. They'll know what to do. If it is a long distance call, call collect. Tell them it's Brian."

Messages from Outer Space

I'm good at biking. It comes with my age. I'm old enough to go places; I'm not old enough to drive a car yet. So the only option is to either have my parents drive me (no way), walk (takes too long) or bike (still cool) — you can almost pretend you *could have* driven yourself but prefer to get the exercise.

Biking from my house to the northern part of town wasn't hard but it took a long time. It was past suppertime; I wondered if they'd found out I was gone yet. Dad, who did most of the cooking, would probably be the one who went looking for me when I hadn't shown up.

I stopped to eat at a small restaurant near the highway, and took my hamburger outside to eat in privacy. Sitting at one of the picnic tables, I pulled my backpack off, and reached inside for the alarm receiver, being careful not to take it all the way out in case someone was watching me. I must have been in a low spot, because even though I was closer to Brian, there was no signal. I needed to get higher. The roof of the restaurant was probably not the best choice.

The North Mountain, on the north side of town, was about a forty-minute climb, straight up by bike. "Real" mountains are much taller and take a lot longer to bike up than forty minutes but the North Mountain was the best I could do. I finished my burger and headed out.

Several times on the way up, I stopped to walk my bike. It was easy to see the road and my surroundings because of the nearly full moon. I pulled out the alarm receiver once along the way, but still there was nothing.

I asked myself what I would do if I got to the top of the mountain and still found no signal. Should I climb a tree? Maybe Brian was further east or west and I should go back down the mountain, and go further west, then head up to the top of Morden Mountain. From peak to peak would take about two hours.

I was at the top when I thought I heard a crackle in my earphones. I stopped the bike and stood beside it, listening, rubbing my fingers across my forehead as I concentrated. Nothing. I started to walk.

The second crackle came as I was guiding my bike onto the gravel off the side of the road. My lungs were already burning from the hike/ride up the mountain. Now it felt like the air was burning as it passed through my throat.

There was no voice, or real sound, just a crackle. I knew I had done the right thing by coming here. If the signal was so weak here all I could get was static, there was no way we would have ever gotten anything at home. The voice transmitter was not even half as powerful as the alarm transmitter.

I pulled my bag off, tore it open and reached for the receiver. The screen lit up like an Indiglo watch. Brian's signal was coming in clearer and stronger than it had since I left my roof. It glowed, in a weird blue light and told me boldly that Brian was definitely to the northeast.

With the alarm signal this strong and the beginnings of something coming in from the voice transmitter, Brian must be somewhere within five to ten miles, as the crow flies.

That narrowed it down to only six or seven other mountains that were within transmitter range of where I was. There was no way I could bike to the top of them all in one night.

Some of these mountain roads weren't paved. There were logging roads, fire roads, four wheeler paths and hiking trails. They branched off all over these mountains, and Brian could be anywhere. I was getting closer. The crackling in my ear proved it, but mostly I could feel it.

There was never any traffic on this road, so I sat down with the alarm receiver on my lap. I stared at it, wishing it could give me something more than a direction. My ears were focused on the earphones.

There was a third crackle. The thought came to me that maybe I should time them, to see if the crackles were coming more often. I looked at my wristwatch: after midnight.

The next crackle came about ten minutes later. Then again, seven minutes later. My ears were telling me that if the crackles were getting stronger, it meant the signal was coming closer. I wasn't moving. So Brian must be.

I jumped to my feet, thinking I needed to be ready for action. Exactly *what* action I didn't know but something was happening and I needed to figure it out fast. The extra two feet from me sitting, to me standing, made the difference. Suddenly, Brian's voice rang out in my ears. I could hear him panting and calling. His voice sounded scared and tired.

He was saying, "SOS somebody, anybody, I need help! Call the police if you can hear this. It's not a joke and I don't have much time. My name is Brian Lutz and my family has been kidnapped. Please, we need help!"

"Brian," I screamed at the top of my lungs, "Can you hear me"!

There was no reply. Brian kept on talking. I wondered how long he had been at it. Had he been calling for help for hours?

I had a receiver, not a transmitter. I could hear Brian, but he had no way of hearing me unless he heard me the old fashioned way. I cupped my hands around my mouth like a megaphone and screamed his name. I realized, with a jolt that shook my body, that his kidnappers obviously couldn't hear him talking into his hat, but they might hear me screaming. What was I thinking? I swore at myself under my breath. I had to think! Use my head!

It was driving me crazy. I could hear him calling for help and no matter what I did I couldn't make his voice transmitter work the other way around.

Then I heard him say something that made my stomach turn. "They changed their minds. Now they are moving us at dawn. You have to stop them or we're all dead."

Jamming everything back into the backpack, I grabbed my bike. I got on and started to peddle as fast as I could. As I sped down the hill, the shadows made by the moonlight seemed to jump out across the road. I was going so fast it was hard to steer. The bike's front wheel shook and wobbled. If I crashed now, Brian and I would both be goners.

I willed Brian to know, or understand, I wasn't leaving him, I was going for help.

The wind made my eyes water. I tried to blink away the tears as they streaked out of my eyes. My shoulders were aching from practically standing on the handlebars. I touched the brakes a little to hold myself back. When I reached the straight stretch at the bottom of the mountain, I let go of the brakes and poured my life energy into my legs with my feet going mad underneath me. With the bike jumping from side to side as it hit small bumps in the road, I fought to keep my balance. Finally, I tucked my head down close over the handlebars and rested my legs on the pedals. I was breathing heavily as I coasted toward town.

As the speed dropped, I again started my crazy peddling. My heart raced and my legs felt like Jello. I was sweating hard but the tears and the wind on my face had made my cheeks so cold they stung.

I had to find a phone! It was faster to call home than it was to bike there. My watch said 12:45; everything was closed by now. Even the convenience stores closed at 11:00.

I turned my bike down a side street to take a shortcut and peddled hard right up to the glowing phone booth outside the convenience store. When I jammed on the brakes my back tire skidded along the pavement out from underneath me.

My legs wouldn't work and my body was tingling all over, as if with tiny electrical shocks. My hands shook so much it was hard to get my wallet out. It took me three tries to slide the coin in the tiny hole.

The answering machine picked up. My father sounded angry, his voice stiff. I'd never heard him sound so worried.

"Andrew, if you hear this message, call your mom's cell."

I dialed the number and Dad answered. "Andrew! Is that you?"

"Yeah, Dad," I panted into the receiver, "It's me."

"Where are you?"

"I'm at the convenience store. Come quick, I've found Brian."

I could hear my mother in the background, asking questions about how I was, but Dad ignored her.

I started to tell them I was sorry I had worried them, but Brian came first. "I got his voice," I said. "The kidnappers were going to lay low for a few days but they changed their minds. They're moving the family as soon as its light. I got radio contact at the top of the North Mountain."

I told them everything I knew. I didn't hang up until I saw the lights of their car pull in the parking lot. We loaded my bike into the trunk and I climbed thankfully into the back seat. We headed for home to grab Mom's laptop and the rest of the tracking equipment we'd need to go and find Brian.

Back into the Lion's Den

New fears came pouring into his head. What would happen to his family if the giant returned to find he had escaped? Would they try to find him, or cut their losses and leave with his mom and dad? Maybe they would kill his parents right then and there.

Pushed on by his new fears, Brian started back down the hill. He hoped he was going the same way he had come. It was easy enough to get lost in the woods in the day. Now that it mattered more than anything in his whole life, Brian looked around to get his bearings.

He felt cold and damp. His throat hurt from calling for help for so long. It was harder going down than up. The moss was now covered with dew, making the ground slippery. He turned his feet sideways to stop sliding. If it had been a cloudy night, he never would've made it.

Brian came into a break in the trees and stopped to catch his breath. Looking around he realized he was standing in the middle of a dirt road. He had missed his target. There had been no road on the way up the hill.

Brian listened to his instincts and turned to the right. Running on the road hurt his swollen feet far more than the moss had. The stars were starting to fade. A dangerous sign that the sun would be rising soon. He had cut it closer than he planned.

The cabin appeared out of nowhere. There were two vans parked in the driveway. Brian ran to the nearest one and dropped to his knees in the dirt. It was his last tool in his bag of tricks and he decided to pull it out now. Pulling the backpack off, he reached inside for the vehicle transmitter. He gave it a shake before sticking it under the bumper. The huge magnet stuck fast to the body of the van.

Brian stayed in a crouched position and moved toward the house. There was no movement inside. With the last of his strength he climbed up on the porch roof. He sat down and put his head between his knees to breathe. He felt a strange urge to roll over and be sick to his stomach.

His mother must have heard him through the open window. He turned at the sound of her whispered voice calling to him. "Brian, hurry, they are going to come for us any minute."

"Hurry! You want me to hurry!" he repeated between gasps. "Boy, I haven't done that in three or four seconds! What was I thinking, lying about, napping and generally being a lazy bum for the past four hours!"

He swallowed hard, trying to wet his dry throat. He knew if he tried to climb, hand over hand, back to the window now, he would fall to the ground. He had to rest a few more minutes.

Finally he stood, his legs still shaky and weak. At least his eyeballs felt like they were back where they were supposed to be and no longer like they were going to bulge out of his head. He grabbed hold of the rain gutter at the edge of the roof and swung toward the bedroom window. After a moment he started moving like a mountain climber — hand over hand, with his feet walking along the wall.

His mother grabbed him by the pajamas and helped pull him over to the window. He lowered himself onto the ledge and down to the floor. She dropped down beside him and hugged him hard. "Quick! We have to get you cleaned up. They're going to know you went out if they find you like this."

She pulled the sheet off the mattress on her cot, and rubbed him down like a wet puppy. After the initial once over, she spent most of her time tending to his feet. They were scratched and bleeding.

Then she bundled up the wet sheet and threw it under the cot. Brian realized her hands were free.

"Hey! You undid your strap!"

She smiled a little. "You're not the only person who can bend, you know. Besides, I was going crazy lying there waiting for you."

"It's a good thing you got them off so you could help me, because after all that running I don't think I would have made it in the window without you," he told her.

This made her smile.

Brian did the straps up behind his mother's back. He told her all he had done in their hours apart. Then he went to the window, shut it and put the slide-bolt back into place. He was about to start putting the screws in when they heard a noise downstairs. His whole body gave a jerk out of fright.

He jumped toward his bed and started to do his straps up. It wasn't tidy, and it wasn't very tight, but it was the best he could do in five seconds or less. Quickly, he worked his hands back under his feet and past his bottom. He and his mother were sitting side by side on Brian's cot when the giant came into the room.

The giant took one look at Brian and asked, "What is wrong with you?"

"I don't feel very good," Brian answered.

"Then you will not mind missing breakfast," he said. "Come on folks, it is time to go."

Again, Brian and his mother were kept separate from his dad. They saw Keith for only a few seconds, as his drugged and limp body was loaded into the other van. There was nothing for any of them to say, so they moved in silence. It felt good to see his dad had not been hurt. The kidnappers were taking very good care of everyone.

The giant urged Brian's mother into the back of the van, helping her balance with her hands fastened behind her. A stocky blond fellow stepped closer as Brian climbed into the van. The man was as calm and confident as an airline attendant waiting for passengers to be seated. Once Brian and his mother were safely stowed inside, the blond man took the seat behind the wheel and the Giant moved into the passenger seat beside him.

The two vans pulled out the driveway as the sun peeked up over the skyline.

Pulling Out

"Andrew," Mom said from the front of the car. "I found the North Mountain on the map. You said you got a good signal from the northwest. I have marked off a ten square mile area for the police to start looking. What do you think? Any gut feelings about this?"

I was staring over her shoulder at the map. Mom had used a red marker to outline the area where the signal could have come from. It gave me a sinking feeling to see all the roads crossing the area. There must have been fifty of them. That didn't include the logging roads, or private roads that led to people's camps or woodlots.

"The search area looks about right to me," I said. "Let's just get going. We've been waiting for everyone to show up for over an hour. If I was going to rob a bank, this is the town I'd do it in. I could sit down, have a cup of coffee in the middle of the robbery, and still get away with it!"

Dad was in the driver's seat. He and Mom looked at each other. "I agree with you son. It should never take this long. I know the local police aren't trained to handle kidnappers but the federal police officer out there sure is."

"Well, what's the holdup?" I snapped.

I knew Dad was trying to calm me down. "The Witness Protection guy seems to be having a hard time organizing the local police force. Look!" he said sitting up straight and tipping his head in the direction of the other cars. "Everyone is at least heading for their cars. It must be time to pull out."

"It's dawn now," I complained. "Brian said they were moving at dawn. Am I the only person who thinks it would've been a better idea to try to find them *before* they started driving? How many times have I heard you say 'a moving target is harder to hit'"

"Yes, but they're not moving yet, are they," Mom said.

"How do you know they aren't?"

"Because you said he had a vehicle transmitter with the motion detector. If Brian has had enough time to turn on the alarm and the voice, then he'd have time to turn on the vehicle transmitter too."

"But there hasn't been a signal from it," I objected. It didn't make any sense.

"The motion detector can tell the difference between the motion of a car and the motion of a person. Brian can shake it all he likes, but it won't start working until it's in a vehicle that moves."

The tracking software was loaded and ready. The map of the area made the computer screen of the laptop glow green, with black lines for roads, grey squares and circles to mark where buildings were. The cellphone receiver was plugged into the cigarette lighter, and an extra long antenna had been stuck on the roof of the car.

The minute the first signal came in, the computer would put a small red dot on the screen's map, showing us exactly where Brian was. When the next signal came in, thirty seconds later, it would put a new dot on the map. From those two dots the computer would be able to tell us if they were moving and how fast they were going.

With the click of the mouse, the computer would automatically show the street name and nearest house numbers. Mom's computer at home could even get the name and phone number of the people who lived in each house you clicked on.

We waited another ten minutes, with the car running, before the police cars pulled out. "Finally," I huffed in frustration.

On The Road

There were no seats in the back of the van, so Brian and his mother were allowed to sit beside one another on the floor, leaning against the side with their hands behind their backs. The windows were made of one way glass.

Brian's pajamas were still damp and he was shivering from the cold. The van had heated up a little since they first climbed in, but not enough to make him comfortable. Warmth wouldn't have helped with the bumps either. Brian could feel every pothole the van drove, through too, and was glad he had slept through the drive in.

They'd been driving for what seemed a long time, moving slowly because of the bad road. It was too narrow to have been a logging road. Big logging trucks never would have made it through.

The van stopped, then made a sharp turn to the left. Here the road was smoother, still a dirt road, but a smoother one. Brian could tell that the van was picking up speed because he saw the trees go by faster. He guessed it was probably around 6:00 in the morning.

Brian jumped as he heard a cellphone ring from the front of the van. The giant, sitting in the passenger seat, pulled the cellphone from a hidden pocket in his pant leg. He spoke so quickly Brian couldn't hear him. Then he snapped the phone shut, returned it to the pocket and leaned over to the driver.

They spoke only briefly before the driver hit the breaks. The van slid over the gravel, tipping slightly as it slowed. Finally, it came to a stop sideways in the road. Working the van forwards and backwards, the driver turned the van around and headed back in the same direction they had come.

Brian watched as the giant opened a bag on the floor, pulled out an earpiece, and fit it into his ear. The box it was attached to had no dials or buttons to select channels, so Brian knew it was a dedicated set. Like walkie-talkies, you turned them both on and they talked together. The small size meant they were only to be used over short distances. The other van must have the match to the pair. They could talk between vans but no one else could overhear them.

Brian and his mother were alone in the back, and Brian felt safe enough to move around. He shifted his weight, so that he could kneel. Looking out the back window, he saw the others catching up to them. He knew it was the van that carried his father. They had been following it out of the woods, now it was following them, back toward the mountains.

The ride was much rougher now. The driver made another sudden turn to the left, and Brian was thrown onto his side. His mother let out a cry, as he banged his head on the steel walls.

The giant glanced over his shoulder, and warned them in his usual deep, thick voice. "You had better stay low back there. The ride is going to get a little bumpier than we had expected."

"Thanks for the warning," Brian said, with a little more sarcasm than he had intended. Then he worked his way carefully toward the center of the vehicle. He was trying to get his head as far away from the hard steel as he could.

They were bouncing crazily down the road. Branches were smashing off the sides of the van. Brian could hear screeching like a cat's claws on a chalkboard as the larger branches scraped along the metal sides. The van rocked dangerously as the driver swerved to the left and to the right trying to avoid potholes.

Every few minutes they would hit a deep and unforgiving pothole. Both Brian and his mother would bounce up in the air as the van leaped into space, only to smash back down. The springs and metal complained loudly, with crunching and banging sounds.

Unable to see where they were going, it came as a surprise when the van swung ninety degrees to the left. Brian's mother let out another loud gasp as the van's back end swung around to the side. The van leaned hard into the turn and threatened to tip completely over but righted itself with a bone jarring snap. The smashing and clanging stopped. Now all they could hear was the quiet hum of the pavement under their tires and the roar of the engine as the van sped down the smooth road.

"You folks all right back there"? a voice from the front called out.

"If you're trying to kill us, you're doing a fine job!" Brian's mother yelled back.

"Mom," pleaded Brian. The last thing they needed was to make these guys mad at them.

There was no need. The giant answered her anyway. "That is not my job madam," he said. "We are being paid to take you to Chicago. What they do with you there is up to them."

Live!

"Signal! Signal! Sweet roses in June, I have a signal," Mom said. It was like a battle cry from the front seat. I had been searching the roads and mountains hoping I would be the one to see the vans.

"Where are they," Dad asked sharply. I stared at his face in the rearview mirror. Dad always stayed calm. He never got upset or excited about anything. Now his voice sounded cold. I felt as if I was seeing a different person sitting there in my father's body. Somehow he seemed bigger.

"They're halfway up Harbourville Mountain," Mom told us. "I can't tell if they are moving or not. I need a second hit to see if the transmitter changes locations."

The same strange voice came out of my father. "Andrew, call the police and tell them we're on Harbourville Mountain. Don't tell them about the transmitter. Just say that we've found a van with Illinois plates and we think it might be them."

It was a lie and I knew it but I had the cellphone in my hand; it had been there since we climbed back into the car at our house. We were a team. It wasn't planned, it just worked out that way. Mom worked the computer, Dad drove the car and I made phone calls.

The local police had given everyone a list of phone numbers to call if we thought we found something. I dialed the first number on the list, and relayed Dad's message. "You don't trust them do you?" I said, once I hung up the phone.

There was silence from the front seat.

"You haven't told them about the GPS transmitter Brian has?" I asked flat out. Again, there was silence. "Yesterday in the kitchen, you wouldn't let me come with you when you talked to the police or that snake guy because you thought I'd talk about the voice transmitter. You don't want them to know because you don't trust them."

Mom spoke up. "You're right. We don't trust them. Not yet anyway."

"Why not?"

"Well," she explained. "You're the one who actually planted the seed. When you and your father discovered the house had been set on fire, you said that the Witness Protection Bureau hadn't done their job very well. The agency is a lot better than that. If things went so terribly, something must be wrong. Something within the system."

This took me by surprise. "I know these guys," she continued in a matter of fact tone. "Not all the people involved in Brian's case of course, but the agency. The agency is full of professionals. They're faster, smarter. It's why they're picked to do what they do."

"You think they're in on it?" I pushed.

"It doesn't matter what I think," she said. "It only matters what I can prove."

"You don't want to prove it by risking Brian," I told her. "You plan on giving everyone the information they need, but you aren't going to tell them how you know. Are you?"

"Well, so much for your dad and me protecting you from the truth," she said with a half smile. "I forget how old you are sometimes. The truth is, none of us would have gotten this far if it hadn't been for you and Brian."

She turned her attention back to the screen. "Three hits! Let's see. Brian's little gang is moving toward us at fifty kilometers per hour. We have to give the police a direction."

Dad was driving the car faster than I had ever gone in a vehicle. He handled the corners like an Indy car driver. It made my heart race. We were about half an hour away from where the signal had started. With any luck one of the police teams might even be closer.

The phone rang once. The local police department dispatcher told us not to try to follow the van ourselves. The police were going to handle it now. The plan was to set up a roadblock at the bottom of the mountain.

Dad ignored the order. He never even took his foot off the gas. We were on the highway and doing well over the speed limit. I realized there wasn't much chance of us getting pulled over by the police. They were all up in the mountains somewhere.

"They're going backwards!" my mother exclaimed. "They turned around; they're headed back up the mountain! Why in the world would they do that?"

"It could be a fluke, " Dad said unconvincingly. "Maybe they have a scanner and heard the police talking about where we're headed and changed directions to avoid us."

My brain screamed and I pressed my fists to my forehead. I knew the answer to what just happened. "Changed their minds! That's it!" I leaned forward in the seat. "Brian said the kidnappers 'changed their minds' late last night and decided to leave at dawn. They'd have no reason to leave early if they didn't think anyone would be looking for them.

"Mom, remember yesterday? You told the police about Keith having a crystal under his skin, and that you picked it up with your bird tracking equipment. The kidnappers found out somehow and knew they had to move him out of radio range. The search was delayed until today so someone could warn the kidnappers before we started looking!"

"You're jumping to conclusions," Mom warned. "It took this long to get organized because the local police force don't have a lot of practice dealing with kidnappings. I'm a little worried about where they're headed now though. If they get out of range of the cellphone towers, we'll lose the signal."

The Informant

"It's ridiculous. There's no way the police *want* Brian's family to be taken away. We can't do this without the police," Dad said. "We have to keep feeding them what we know; we can't tell them *how we know it*. Most of them are still on our side.

We know there has to be an informant. That's how they've been keeping ahead of us. "Whoever it is," he steamed, "I want to catch the little rat with my bare hands, but catching him isn't the most important thing. We have to figure out a way of getting around him. How do we stop an informant inside the police department and still use the same department. Anybody have any ideas?"

"I don't think our informant is in the police department. There is no reason anyone on the local police department would know the Lutzs were in the Witness Protection Program. It wouldn't happen. It has to be someone from inside the program."

"Look, they turned off the road, I said, pointing to the computer screen. "It looks like they're driving through the woods. It must be Brow Mountain Road. It was upgraded from a logging road but still hasn't made it onto all the maps. The kidnappers are going way too fast for anything else."

Mom zoomed out on the map so we could get a better idea of where they were headed. "It looks like it could be a connecting road," Dad said. "I think they were heading for the Provincial Highway in the first place. Unless they stop all of a sudden, my guess is they'll turn right again. It will bring them back down off the mountain and onto the highway. Short of an airplane, the highway's the fastest way out of the province."

"We haven't told the police they've turned around yet! What if we tell the police one thing and tell that snake guy something different? How would it work?"

"No good," Mom said. "If Don Proctor is the informant he'll know where the kidnappers are going. He'll know we're sending him the wrong way."

"Exactly! Look, if we send this Proctor guy off in the wrong direction, and he is in on it, he'll know it's the wrong way, and go along with it. Then we can call the regular police and feed them the real information, on the QT."

I looked over our list of phone numbers and found the number listed for the NAIPA agent who had slithered into our house through the back door. In the deepest part of me I knew he was the one we were working against.

To make it more official we decided Mom should be the one to make the call. Mom quickly told him where we were *not* going.

I dialed the numbers and handed the phone to Dad. He had slowed the car down but we were still speeding. Dad told the officers that Proctor was thinking the kidnappers must have a police scanner and were listening in on our conversations. For security reasons we were going to use cellphones. All further information would be coming from our family. They shouldn't call Proctor directly.

He warned them that in case the kidnappers were still trying to listen in, Proctor was going to keep talking to us through the police channels, but it was a decoy. We were all supposed to pretend to go along with what he said.

Just as Dad had guessed, the little red dots on the computer screen turned right when they met with the Old Weston road. The kidnappers were headed back down the mountain toward the Provincial Highway.

Proctor's voice came over the scanner. He asked each of the cars to report their locations. One by one, the police reported back fake locations. They had all been listening to one another's answers, and simply picked a different road up in the mountains when it was their turn. It sounded very natural.

Proctor told everyone he thought he had a visual. "They're moving south on Brooklyn Street. I need some backup."

Two cars radioed back, saying they would try to get ahead of the vans, using different roads and try to box the van in, then force it to stop.

As soon as the radio chatter stopped, I started dialing Dad's cellphone again. I told each one of the police officers we knew exactly where the van was located, how fast it was going and in what direction. They asked if we had a visual. I lied and said we did, even though we were still one kilometer behind the kidnappers.

I knew there was no point in driving up to the van. It wasn't like we could drive up beside them, and make a peace sign out the window. They weren't about to pull over, hand over the Lutz family and shake hands with us on a job well done.

We drove in silence for ten or fifteen minutes, before the sound of Proctor's voice came through the scanner. Again he was calling all cars to report their locations.

The first two gave a street and a direction. The third car reported their own location as being at a set of lights on the corner of Taylor and Rose.

"The Devil you are!" screamed Proctor's voice over the airwaves. "I'm at the corner of Taylor and Rose. There isn't another car within miles of here. Now, where in Hades are you?"

There was silence as the officer tried to figure out what to say. He hadn't got the response he had been expecting.

"Busted," Mom whispered.

"The regular force guys have got to be close to us by now," Dad said reaching for the police scanner. He put the microphone to his mouth, as the confused officer began to speak. Dad interrupted him.

"Okay everyone. It is time to come clean. We have to . . . "

"Come clean about what!" Proctor demanded.

" . . . come up with a plan to stop these guys, and not hurt the cargo," Dad continued. "I don't know what kind of gas tank those vans have, but they will have to . . . "

"All cars report your locations!" screamed Proctor. "Johnston, get off the air!"

" . . . pull over sooner or later," Dad continued as if he hadn't even spoken. "How does everyone feel about waiting until they pull over and then take them by surprise?"

"All cars," Proctor said in a slightly quieter voice. He was trying to take control of the situation. Screaming hadn't worked, so now he was trying again, with an authoritative voice. "I repeat! All cars, report your exact locations."

There was a short silence. Then one of the patrol cars spoke up. "We're just pulling onto the highway, at exit seventeen. We have a visual contact. There are two vans, driving bumper to bumper in front of me, about twenty meters. They both have Illinois plates and tinted windows. These are our boys. We're traveling in a ghost car, but I'm going to drop back so they don't ID me."

He stayed on the line but his voice changed. It was challenging, and a bit edgy. "*Exactly where are you, Mr. Witness Protection Program?*" he asked.

The Fox

B rian still had no idea where they were other than that they were headed out of the mountains. He kept trying to see past the trees to find a landmark.

Maybe putting the tracking transmitter under the van had not been such a good idea? What if it had bounced off, or got scraped off, when they went smashing through the woods? What could he use to call for help now? He looked around the van.

There was very little he could do with his hands tied behind his back. If he could think of a good reason to have his hands un-strapped, what could he do then? It wasn't as though he could pull one of the transmitters out of his bag and pop a few new batteries into it. Where would he get a watch battery? If he could get one he could replace the dead batteries in the voice transmitter and call for help again.

The phone in the front of the van rang for the second time. Again, both Brian and his mother jerked at the sound.

The giant and the driver looked at one another. They seemed as surprised as Brian had been. Then the giant answered the phone. He was still wearing his headgear and had to adjust it quickly to use the cellphone. Brian could hear only one side of the conversation. Brian's clothes were dry now and he should have been warm, but the phone call made him shiver.

"Go ahead," the giant barked. There was a short silence, followed by, "what kind of transmitter!"

The Hound

Mom grabbed the microphone to the scanner. "They took the off-ramp to Berwick," she said. "Maybe they are headed in for gas."

"I thought you said you were staying a kilometer back," somebody asked.

"We are," she said.

"Then how do you know they took the off-ramp into Berwick?" he asked.

"Bird tracking equipment," she answered, without missing a beat. "Keith has a quartz crystal implanted in his skin, and I was able to pick it up on my bird tracking equipment."

"Holy cats lady," a voice exclaimed over the scanner. "You should be selling this stuff to the police, not the wildlife guys!"

If the situation hadn't been so serious, we probably would have laughed. Instead we all held on tight as Dad cut the wheel hard to the left to avoid driving into the back end of the car ahead of us. Then he cut hard to the right, to get back into our own lane.

The Bird

Brian could feel all the blood leaving his face. His heart stopped beating as fear gripped his chest and squeezed it, without mercy. The world around him started to go dark. He could feel himself slipping away. The last thing he heard before he fainted was the far-off sound of his mother's loving voice.

When the sound came back, it was loud. It seemed far away, but somehow it reminded him of thunder. Maybe he had died and was now in Valhalla, the great hall where Viking warriors went when they died a hero's death. Struck down in the heat of battle. He'd been struck down in battle, hadn't he? His family was at war. They had the transmitters tucked away in his backpack and he had lost the battle. It counted, didn't it?

Maybe the sound that kept booming inside his head was Thor, the Viking God of Thunder. Whatever it was, it was getting closer. Now, he could feel it vibrating in his chest as well as in his head.

Slowly the blackness around him began to clear. It seemed strange he had forgotten, briefly, that he even knew how to see. It was almost deflating that the voice hadn't been Thor's. He knew now, with a crushing weight, it belonged to the giant.

Brian's hands had been untied, and the big man had a hold of him by the shoulders. He realized he was being shaken. "*(Where is the transmitter under your father's skin)?*" The words didn't make any sense.

Again, the kidnapper shook him and yelled the same question into his face. "Spit it out! The transmitter under your father's skin . . . where is it"?

Brian was confused and shaken. "The transmitters aren't under his skin. I don't know what you're talking about," he blurted, in a spike of panic. Brian realized his hands were on the man's chest as he tried to push him away. The giant shook him again and Brian snapped his head around to look for the backpack. He could no longer feel it on his back.

The bag was lying near his mother. The giant had untied his hands and taken off the backpack when he realized Brian had fainted.

"Tell me where they implanted the transmitter on your father so we can get rid of it," the giant boomed red faced.

Brian stared at him, as if he were out of his mind. Brian was missing a huge piece of this puzzle and knew it. Was this was something his father had told them? If he said the wrong thing, would they start skinning his father like a rabbit to get rid of the transmitter? Was this part of someone's plan to rescue them?

Brian decided they all needed to get someplace public. It would be much harder to skin his dad alive downtown in a city than it would be out here in the middle of the country. He had an idea. If they were going to kidnap his whole family, then ask him questions about his father, they could darn well expect him to lie.

All was fair in love and wrestling.

He knew he had slipped up a moment earlier and thought maybe his truthful little slipup could be made to work for them, instead of against his dad.

"It's not under his skin," he blurted out. "It's something he has to swallow every Monday. It takes about a week for him to pass it through his body. It works fine, out here in the open. Where it doesn't work is in a town or city. All the radio and electrical signals kind of drown it out."

The kidnapper let go of him, as if he were a hot potato, and thundered to the front seat. Brian hoped he would be able to overhear the next conversation, but road noise and his mother's crying made it impossible to hear anything other than a mumble.

"Is it true," she asked him with tears swelling in her eyes. "Does your father swallow transmitters and he's never told me?"

It took Brian a few seconds to realize his Mother wasn't joking. "No, Mom," he said in a whispered hiss. "I had to tell them something didn't I? I lied. Dad doesn't have a transmitter under his skin, either. I told them that to get us off this highway. The last thing we want is to actually get to Chicago."

"I had no idea what he was talking about," his mother confessed. "Then he went over to you. I had no idea what had happened to you. I feel so out of control. We're never going to make it!"

"Listen," said Brian, trying to calm her down. "If they're looking for transmitters, they must know we're being followed. It can only mean one of the transmitters worked. We got a signal through. Our friends and the police are looking for us. The mob knows it and now so do you and I."

It took a few minutes to sink in, but when it did she closed her eyes, let out a long deep breath and leaned back against the side of the van.

Suddenly the back half of the van slid out to the right as if it were racing around to catch up with the front half. The van did a half turn and the slide stopped with a jerk as the front half took over the lean once more. It was as if carpet had been ripped out from underneath them. As soon as he caught his balance, Brian climbed to his knees to see where they were. Grabbing the sides of the van he looked out the front window and read the sign for Berwick. They were about three hours away from home.

Then he turned to look out the back window. He half expected to see Andrew grinning at him through the windshield of the Johnson's family car. He wasn't there. The van carrying his father was less than ten feet behind him. He had the sudden urge to wave.

"It's okay, Mom, Dad is right behind us," he said turning to his mother. She nodded her head but she kept her eyes shut tight.

Brian inched his way toward the front. They were coming up to a stop sign and had started to slow down. If they stopped at the sign, he could jump out. His hands were already free. The door was right there in front of him. The giant was busy. Then what? he wondered.

Brian's brain began racing, spinning with the possibilities. If he made a run for it, would they shoot him? He looked up at the front of the van where the kidnappers sat. If he did make it out, the giant could catch him in seconds. Maybe it would create a diversion and give whoever was following them a chance to do something. But what?

No, he decided. This was not the right place. His legs felt weak by the time he finally made up his mind not to make a run for it. It was a relief when the van came to a full stop, and then quickly turned in toward town. They rolled away from the stop sign, as the Johnstons started up the off-ramp.

The Dog

Mom glanced up at Dad as we were coming up the ramp behind the two vans. Both vans had stopped and we were gaining on them quickly. "We're getting a little close aren't we." It wasn't a question, but I didn't give him time to answer.

"No," I said. "The kidnappers don't know who we are, so maybe we can get close enough to let Brian see us. Then he'll know we're here. It might give us an advantage."

The Cat

We had driven into Kentville many time before and I knew it was a little over ten minutes from the off-ramp to town.

"Let's pass these guys," Dad said. "If they think they're being followed they'll be looking in the rear-view mirror. They won't be paying attention to who is in front of them. We know where they're going. None of the roads between here and Kentville go anywhere. They all feed back to the main street so the only place the kidnappers *can* go is straight into town. I think we should get there first."

"It is a lot harder to track someone when you're in front of them," Mom warned " but I think it's worth a try."

"Yeah," I chimed in. "Let's get ahead of them."

I felt a knot in the middle of my chest as we pulled up beside the first van. In my imagination I was expecting to see Brian staring out the window. He would see me as our car passed them. A look of surprise would come over his face. I would give him the "okay" hand signal. Then he would nod his head to let me know he understood, and we would drive past.

It didn't happen. Things almost never happen the way you imagine.

Instead I stared at tinted windows that reflected only the sky and white clouds. There was no way to know if Brian had seen us. I snapped my head around and tried to look casual. My spine was frozen into place.

"Mirrored windows," I heard Dad say. "Nice touch." It was not a voice of praise, but of anger.

I glanced up at the second van a few times as we passed it, still trying to catch Brian's attention and seem casual at the same time. As we pulled back into the right lane, I felt my body relax, knowing that the kidnappers couldn't see me anymore. My hand had been gripping the door handle for so long my fingers were white. My head throbbed from holding my breath for so long. My skin was tingling and my upper lip was damp from nervous sweat.

"If these kidnappers are talking to someone on our side they are going to find out pretty soon we've followed them off the highway," I said. "Maybe we can use it to herd them someplace. You know, a little false information, or something."

"Great minds think alike," Dad said. "The problem is, we don't want to send the police off on a wild goose chase. Because when we really need them they'll be too far away."

"Let's get the kidnappers running first," Mom said, grabbing the microphone to the radio. She clicked the button and started talking to the other police officers. "Heads up guys. I have to warn you about something. The bird tracking system we have doesn't work very well in and around buildings. The signal bounces off the flat walls and confuses the receiver. The absolute worst place for these kidnappers to go is downtown, around the park. If the kidnappers start driving in circles we could lose them, so everyone keep a careful eye out."

Mom put the microphone down and Dad drove to the center of town and pulled over.

From where we were sitting, we could see everything in the park to our left. We had a clear view both up and down the street we were on. In addition, we were parked at the intersection, so we could see up the street to our right. Dad grabbed the computer, and pulled up the built-in map. The computer zoomed out to show a bigger picture of Kentville and the area around it.

The message didn't take long to get relayed. The red dot on the screen turned off the main road into town and went down a side street. The radio came alive as the first police car reported they had seen the car turn right on Roscoe Drive.

We watched the computer screen as the dot turned left and then a quick right on the very next street. One police car called in to say they had lost sight of the vans. Dad grabbed the cellphone and called one of the police officers. After a quick conversation, they agreed that two police cars would stay on the chase and the rest of the cars would gather near the park. We were going to set up a trap and take them down.

I wondered what Brian was doing right now.

The Mouse

"Hang on!" Brian yelled at his mother. Her eyes were as wide as an owl's at midnight. For the second time she had been caught off guard by a sharp turn and thrown toward the back of the van.

"Hang on to what," she snapped "My other hand?"

Brian had not seen the Johnstons as they had driven past the van. He had been crouched down low, behind the Giant's seat, trying to overhear what was being said. This time when the cellphone rang he braced himself for more bad news.

The Giant's voice rang out loud and clear. "The police cannot track us in and around tall buildings. We can lose the police by weaving around the streets near the center of town. That's where most of the tall buildings are. Then head for the old highway."

Within a moment, the van swung to the right. Brian lost his footing and slammed into the steel wall again. His head struck hard and the sound of squealing tires mixed with the ringing in his head. He was halfway across the floor moving toward his mother when it made a wild swing to the left. This time Brian crashed headlong into his mother's knees. They weren't as hard as the steel but still not his idea of a soft landing.

"We're sliding around like a pair of crazy carpets back here!" Brian exclaimed. "If you are going to keep driving like this, can I undo my mother's hands so she can hang on?"

The giant glanced over his shoulder. "No! Your hands should be tied up right now too, but I am a little busy. For now, you will have to hang on for the both of you."

Brian sat down beside his mother and put one hand across her chest to hold her back. He braced himself with his other hand. It was lucky he was still in bare feet, he thought, as he planted them out flat in front of him. His mother had done the same. For the next twenty minutes they did nothing but hang on as the van swerved wildly from one side of the road to the other, skidding around hairpin turns.

"Are there no police at all in Kentville?" Brian asked his mother sarcastically. He didn't want to draw any attention from the giant. He seemed a fairly nice fellow — for a kidnapper — but right now he was a little on edge. "Maybe they have different driving laws in Kentville. I got a ticket in Chicago for skateboarding on the sidewalk. These guys have been drag racing everywhere and not a single cop has shown up. What kind of lawless town is this?"

Brian's mother smiled at his ability to make a joke even in the most stressful situations. It was cut short as they were both thrown toward the back as the driver gunned the engine.

The Hunter

Once Dad had hung up the phone, we headed for the park at the center of town. We pulled up by the curb and stopped. I was watching the dot on the screen when Dad cut the engine and jumped out of the car. I started to follow. Mom reached into the back seat. "Stay right where you are."

"Why, what's going on?" I asked.

"The kidnappers are heading into this town square," Mom explained. "You and I are going to watch the screen. We need to tell the police which road the kidnappers are coming in on so they'll be able to set up a controlled takedown. We have eight officers ready to jump out and stop them as soon as they enter the square."

"What if they don't stop?" I asked. "What if they keep driving?"

"Then we'll shoot their tires out," she said very matter-of-factly. "They'll either stop or crash. There's usually minimal damage to passengers." Sensing my shock, she turned to me. "No matter how you shake it Andrew, this is dangerous. We're trying to end it as safely as possible, but nothing is guaranteed."

Mom and I waited in our car and watched the screen. The little red dot turned left on one street, to turn right on the next. It made big circles to double back and get behind anyone who might be following. It didn't take long before it was heading toward us.

Mom picked up the cellphone and made the call. I ignored the dot as I watched the police directing people back into buildings before they took their positions behind parked cars or the raised cement planters that lined the park. They were crouched down low, their rifles positioned, ready to fire.

When I looked back to the park, I saw it was empty. Mom and I sat, waited, and studied the screen. It felt as if I was watching a movie about a ghost town, where time went by in slow motion. We watched the dot coming into the town square from the road to our right. I realized in horror I was about to get a clear view of the shootout at the OK Corral with Brian's family right in the middle of it.

The Hunted

Brian heard the phone ring again, but was too busy trying to keep his mother and himself from getting smashed around to pay attention. There was a shout from the front seat and the driver jammed on the brakes. The tires screeched in protest and sent up a cloud of bad smelling smoke. The van came to a stop.

Both Brian and his mother held their breath. They waited for the van behind them to slam into their bumper. The driver cranked the wheel to the right and hit the gas pedal hard. The engine roared to life. The tires squealed once more. The weaving up and down side streets and driving in circles ended. Now they were racing. Every few minutes they swung in and out of the oncoming traffic as they passed any vehicle doing less than Mach 1. Dread filled Brian's soul when he realized they were headed back toward the mountains.

The Bear

The vans appeared up the side street and headed for the square in front of us. I felt helpless just sitting there watching them head toward us, the roadblock and the soon-to-be gunfire. Then, without warning, the nose of the van dipped down and smoke poured out from its tires as they skidded along the pavement. I thought for a second the van was on fire, that one of the police officers had shot the tires. The back part of the vehicle started to slide out to the side. It jerked quickly, then changed direction and disappeared up a side street. The second van followed the first.

We looked back down at the computer screen. The red dot gave up its blindfolded hamster dance around the screen. Confused, we waited to see if they were going to turn back. Maybe try a different way into the square. They didn't. They were traveling faster and faster, *away* from us.

The officers had been watching for them, the same as we were. We all saw the vans turn down the side street. The officers stood up, waiting for some signal from us about where the kidnappers were headed now. Jumping out of the car I waved my hands and yelled, "They're on to us! They're heading for the mountains!"

Dad left his position with the other officers and was back in the car before I was and we were racing again to catch up to Brian. Dad had picked up the phone and called the Department of Highways. I heard Dad say we were planning on driving over the North Mountain. Dad asked if there were any abandoned logging roads on the current map that went over the mountains but were no longer maintained.

They told Dad not to take the Lightfoot Trail because the bridge was out.

Dad thanked the man and hung up. He'd made the decision to send the kidnappers up the Lightfoot Trail. It was time to start playing dirty. We were going to set up our own ambush. We knew exactly where the vans were. This time we weren't telling.

The Honey

"I'll call Donny. I know we can trust him, he's been a police officer in Aylesford for his whole life. If we can trust anyone, we can trust him.

"Hi Donny," Mom said moments later. "I have a gut feeling that I know where these guys are headed. Remember this has *got to be* between you and me."

Donny laugh so loud we could all hear him. "If your gut feeling is any indication of woman's intuition, then you have all the men on this police force at a serious disadvantage and we should go the heck home," he told her. "You are just plain spooky."

Mom smiled. "These guys are aiming for the old highway, using the fire roads. They're going to make a run for it, up over the Lightfoot Trail. It's a dirt road that starts out fine but the going will be slow. If you can take one of the paved roads across you should have time to circle around. There's a bridge out, about three-quarters of the way across. It can act as a roadblock and you can meet them head-on there. The rest of us can box them in from behind."

Again there was silence on our end. Donny told Mom they were heading over the mountains. Mom hung up the cellphone and picked up the police radio. "Okay men," I heard her say. "I can't track these guys in the mountains. We'll have to divide up. Each of us take a different mountain pass." She gave each police team a different road. No one was given the road past Lake Blake. The kidnappers would also hear her message. Hopefully they would fall for it. I didn't need to ask which road we were going to be on. I didn't know the name but I knew it went past Lake Blake.

The Nut

The giant was busy with the map and the cellphone. Brian had lost track of how many times the phone had rung. They were well into the mountains when both vehicles suddenly stopped. This time the giant jumped out and ran to the van behind them. Brian watched out the window as his father was lifted out of the van. He was being carried by the giant and a second man Brian had only seen briefly this morning.

The side door of their van was opened. Brian's mother gasped as she saw her husband being lowered onto the floor in front of her. The new guy climbed in the back and slammed the door closed behind him. He was very muscular, but not in the same way the giant was. He was lean and wiry, like a stretched out rubber band just ready to snap. You could see the muscle groups in his face move when he flexed his jaw. The look he gave Brian as he sat and placed his gun across his knees was not a look of kindness. He pulsed with an air of annoyed and angry energy. Mr. Grumpy was not going to be anybody's friend today.

When the giant was in the passenger seat once more, they headed off deeper into the woods. Glancing out the rear window, Brian lost sight of the second vehicle as it disappeared onto another dirt road.

Brian turned his attention to his drugged father on the floor. There was nothing he could do for him right now. Once again Brian tried to figure out the reason why the kidnappers had split up. Was it a good sign or a bad one?

Brian and his mother had been trying to stay upright the whole time they bumped and bounced through the woods. Every so often the engine would roar as the van took flight and leapt into the air before it came down with a vision-blurring impact, back onto the road. They never stood a chance when the van slammed on its brakes and stopped inches away from what used to be a bridge. Both were sent tumbling into the back of the front seats.

The Squirrel

Once we left the main road it got more than a little bumpy. "I don't believe it!" screamed my mother from the front seat. "They've turned! There is no way they could have known we were behind them! What have they got, for Pete's sake, a tracking system on *us*?"

Dad slammed his hand down on the steering wheel. "Is it a through road?" he asked.

Mom clicked on the computer for a second. "Yes," she said. "It goes all the way through. It comes out on the old highway. I'll call Donny again. This can still work. There won't be a roadblock. He'll have to make one."

"Donny won't be able to do it by himself," I said. "They're either going over the trail or coming back down the way they came. It's safe to tell the officers where they are so they can come in as backup."

"He's right," Dad said. "Call Donny and the rest of them. It's time we brought this thing to an end. We're going to box them in. Andrew, you get on the phone."

I dialed the list and explained. I was staring out the window, watching the trees. We reached the Y in the road, where the red dot had turned off, away from the Lightfoot Trail. I saw tire tracks heading off in the other direction. If I hadn't been on the phone, talking and thinking at the same time, I might have said something, but I didn't. I looked at the computer screen to see how far behind we were. "Why have they stopped?" I asked a little too loud.

The Ambush

The driver slammed on the brakes and dropped the van into park. Everything he would need was on the seat beside him. The bomb had been put together days ago. He grabbed it and opened his door. Using the door as a brace, he slid underneath in one quick movement and dropped the bomb on the ground under the gas tank.

Pulling the pin on the two-minute timer, he climbed back out and started to run down the road in the same direction he had been headed. The bang would be huge and he needed as much space between him and the upcoming explosion as possible. The driver also knew that if he was still being followed there was no way the police would be able to get past the burning remains. Their vehicles would be stopped cold.

Police procedure would be to start looking for anyone who might be on foot. They would start at whatever was left of the vehicle, then spread out, in bigger and bigger circles, looking for footprints. If he ran straight down the road for a few hundred meters before heading into the woods it would give the driver a head start before the police started finding his footprints — perhaps enough time for him to get to the end of the Lightfoot Trail and meet up with the first van.

Big Bang Theory

If Dad hadn't taken his foot off the gas we would have blown up right along with the van. We came around the last corner and saw it for a split second before it turned into a pulsing ball of flames. The first explosion lifted it ten feet into the air. A second ripped it into a dozen pieces, sending glass, metal and flames in every direction.

I could feel the blast from each explosion, as if someone very large was trying to push the air out of my lungs. The bushes, trees and grass closest to the blast were all blown flat. Small fires were burning where puddles of gas had caught the grass.

The main part of the van came back down to earth, like a huge fiery skeleton. It was roaring at us not to get too close. "Now what?" I whispered.

"We wait for backup," Dad answered. While we waited my imagination was left to run wild as to who or what had been inside the van when it blew. The hopeful part of my brain told me maybe the Lutzs were in the other van speeding down the road ahead of this one.

The first van was not, however, headed happily down the road on the other side of the fiery pile of burning steel. It had run into a small problem of its own. The road it had taken to Lake Blake was missing a bridge and there was no way to get a van through the gully without the bridge there.

Dad and Mom both stepped out as soon as the first police car arrived. "They want to investigate this crime scene first," my father explained through the driver's window. "There could be clues here we can't miss. We don't know for sure where the other van is. They could have separated anywhere. We don't even know if anyone got out of this one or not. If they did, the kidnappers could be sitting in a tree somewhere waiting to shoot us.

"Stay in the car until we know the coast is clear. I am very proud of you. But you are still my son, and I'm ordering you to stay here, in the car, until we know it is safe."

I waited until Mom and Dad had walked away, then jumped out, grabbed my bike out of the trunk and headed back down the road toward the Y. Dad had always told me to trust my instincts. So, in a sense, this was his fault. I knew without any question the Lutzs weren't in the woods. They had taken the Y in the road and I wasn't waiting for anyone else to go after them.

My legs pumped hard at the pedals. In less than half an hour I had found the van. If the kidnappers were still inside they wouldn't have heard me coming; the woods were a great muffler of sound. As soon as I saw a flash of colour through the trees, I slid the bike quietly into some bushes, then circled around through the woods on foot.

Rising slowly out of the underbrush I studied the van. There was no movement anywhere. They had parked the van in front of a gully. The broken timbers were all that was left of what had once been a bridge.

I took a deep breath and started looking around. I knew deep down that the whole "*I was just doing what you told me to do! Following my instincts, Dad*" thing, was never going to save my hide. He was going to let me have it when he finally found me.

The Rat

It was at least a small comfort that Mr. Grumpy in the rear of the van wasn't doing any better than Brian's family were. He was also caught off guard and went charging uncontrollably toward the front seat. Keith Lutz's drugged form rocked forward and slid into the rest of passengers like a bowling ball.

The kidnappers knew there was no going back. This was a one-way trip. The driver shut the van off and climbed into the cargo area. Mr. Grumpy flung open the side door and climbed out, his gun held ready to go, in one hand.

Mr. Grumpy grabbed Brian by the front of his pajamas and half dragged him out. The driver had a hold on his mother. He was more gentle with her as he half pushed, half dragged her out of the van. Brian had no chance to grab his backpack. The batteries were dead by now anyway.

Jerked forward by the large hand gripping his shoulder, Brian was shoved toward his mother. The hand squeezed tighter to show Brian he was supposed to get into line behind her. When they made into the woods, Brian and his mother were between the driver and Mr. Grumpy. Brian looked back to see his comatose father lifted onto the giant's shoulder. The giant's face showed no sign of effort.

Brian's mother stumbled and crashed into him. He caught her before she hit the ground. The driver also reached out to help. "Look," Brian said. "We don't have shoes or clothes. Can my mother at least have her hands free?"

"Good point kid," said the driver, as he ripped the strap off of her hands. "I'm sorry ma'am." Brian realized it was the first time he had heard the driver's voice clearly. It had been a mumble from the front seat until now.

Mr. Grumpy growled from behind them. There was no question about who was in charge when he said, "Now your hands are free, maybe you can walk a little faster." He gave Brian a shove to get him moving again. Brian used his left hand to hold his mother's and follow the new guy further into the woods.

Brian could feel that help was close. He couldn't fight these men in black and win, but he wouldn't follow them either. He had to do something. A branch caught Brian in the face. The pain in his lip made him forget he was afraid. "Don't they have boy scouts on your planet!" he yelled. "If a branch is in your way, it's going to be in my way too. You don't snap branches back at the guy behind you. You break it, or hold it!"

Mr. Grumpy was not nice. "You think the branches should be broken, *you* break them," he said, driving his pointer finger into Brian's chest. Their faces were inches apart. Mr. Grumpy turned away and kept walking.

With one hand pressed to his swelling lip and the other rubbing the sore spot in his chest where he had been poked, Brian had an idea. These were city guys. None of them had ever been in the woods. Heck, Brian thought, a year ago I'd never been in the woods either.

If he broke branches along the path, it would be easier for the police to follow them. It might save them time catching up. Chicago policemen know how to get around in the city. Put them in the country, and they'd be in trouble. Brian wondered briefly if country policemen had to take a course in wilderness tracking.

Holding his mother's hand with his left, Brian started to walk a little slower than before. He reached out with his right hand, which was free, and snapped off a branch that came close to his face. No one noticed.

On Foot

Quickly I checked to see if anything had been left behind. In the corner lay Brian's backpack. My breath burst from my body like a geyser. I climbed in to see what else I could find.

The keys were in the ignition and there was a cellphone on the floor. I picked up the phone and called my folks. There was no answer. I left a message and tried one of the police officer's phone numbers I had dialed earlier. He answered.

"This is Andrew," I said. "I found the other van. It's about five miles up the road to Lake Blake. It's empty but I found Brian's backpack."

"We're on our way. We should be there in less than fifteen minutes," the voice had said. "Don't go anywhere near the van. I mean it!"

Of course I wasn't going to go anywhere near it. I was done with it. Now I needed to be near the kidnappers and my friend. Wherever they were headed, I was going, too.

I dropped the phone without hanging it up, grabbed the car keys in case they doubled back, and shoved them into my pocket. As a second thought, I grabbed Brian's backpack, slipped it into position on my back, and buckled it up.

The kidnappers had a head start on me and I needed to figure out how many people were out there. If I knew how many tracks there were to begin with, then I would know if someone veered off. They had split up once and might do it again. It was also possible they might send one person to double back and see if they were being followed.

I wanted to catch up but I did not want them to catch up with me. I was no good to anyone if I got caught, too.

The first trail leading into the woods had been made by just one person. There was one large footprint of a square-toed work boot pressed into a trampled down fern. There were no other prints around it.

The second trail had more activity including two sets of marks from bare feet. One set of prints had baby toes that didn't leave a mark, making it look like an eight-toed person.

It came to me like a wave of white heat over my face. Brian and his family had been taken at night. They didn't put their shoes on before they left the van because they didn't have any shoes *to* put on! Barefoot hostages were definitely going to slow these guys down.

Then I saw two more sets of workboot marks. I knew it was two pairs because they were walking side by side for a brief time. I was surprised to see how big the square-toed mark was. It was much deeper than all the others. I stepped into it for an idea how big it was. It was almost one and a half times the size of my foot, and I wear a size nine! This guy was *big*.

The trail was easy to follow — covered with broken branches and ferns — leading clearly into the woods. They were far enough away that I didn't have to worry about being heard. I broke into a run.

The further I ran, the more I began to realize someone was trying to leave me a trail. There were too many branches being broken in places where they shouldn't have been. There was some damage on the left side of the path but mostly on the right. I found a twig the size of my thumb that had been snapped off. They had been left hanging at shoulder height, like flags for anyone who might come from behind.

Brian was right handed. I smiled at the thought of him walking along in bare feet trying to be casual about breaking so many branches. He must have thought I was either completely blind or a pathetically bad tracker. We'd have to talk about this later.

The ground was typically uneven. Whenever I came to the top of a rise I stopped to listen and to count footprints. Five . . . five . . . always five. They hadn't set up a lookout. It was a good sign that they weren't expecting company.

It was well into the afternoon when I saw the first movement. It scared me a little, so I ducked down and got flat on my stomach.

The kidnappers were trying to walk in a straight line away from the van, using the sun as a compass. They were keeping their backs to the sun as a way of getting out of the woods, but as the sun moved in the sky they ended up making a wide circle to the east. They weren't nearly as far away from the van as they thought they were.

I waited until the last person disappeared over the next rise. There were six people in total. Three dressed in black. It was going to make it much harder to follow them at night.

Brian and Mrs. Lutz were walking. Mr. Lutz was being carried fireman style, over the shoulder of the last man in black. It explained why the square-toed print had been so deep. He was carrying an extra body.

I thought about waiting there until Dad and the others caught up. The part of my brain in charge of keeping me safe told me it was the best idea. Getting back to my feet slowly, I decided to listen to the *other* part of my brain. It was telling me to stay close to my friend. Yes, help was on the way, but who knew what might happen between now and then. The trail was easy enough to follow. Dad should catch up soon. Even sooner, depending on how angry he was.

Being within sight of them, I decided to leave their path. I didn't want them to turn around and see me. My stomach growled and I realized I hadn't had anything to eat since my hamburger last night. I couldn't run through the woods forever with nothing in my stomach. Running a loop around them would give me a chance to find some food.

As a kid, camping had been strictly a "Dad and the Lad" event for us. Mom hated to rough it. When she went camping we slept under the five stars of the Hilton. Dad was the opposite. He would rather live off whatever the forest around us had to offer, than pack in a cooler full of store-bought stuff.

I knew what you could eat in the woods. Most plants were fine but some could do really weird things to you. Some could even kill you. No cure, no chance; it's that simple. After running in a wide loop around the kidnappers and Brian's family, I found a good spot to find some food. Having a father who was an environmental biologist had its benefits. There was a patch of chanterelle mushrooms under a birch tree, so I sat down beside them. The backpack was getting heavy. I slipped it off, picked a few handfuls of mushrooms and ate them right away. They smelled wonderfully like apricots.

After eating a few, I opened the bag and started collecting extras. It was light enough that I could still see the difference between the light yellow mushrooms in the middle of the patch and the darker orange mushrooms of the false chanterelle that usually surround them.

I knew they wouldn't kill me, but didn't have either the time or the bathroom that would be necessary if I got them confused. A few times I had to smell them to double-check the good ones from the bad ones. The false ones don't smell sweet.

I could hear Brian's group coming in my direction through the woods. I waited for them to pass by me so I could start following them again. I would have to move carefully and keep low to the ground, if I was going to stay beside them. People never look beside them when they think they are being followed. Especially when it was starting to get dark.

The kidnappers kept getting closer. I realized too late that they weren't going to follow the natural lay of the land. Instead they were going to fight against it and walk into the lowest gully around so they could fight to walk right back up out of it. These were definitely not boy scouts.

There was no chance of me backing away without being seen. If you can't run, you can always hide, I told myself. After a quick glance around I found the best chance I had and went for it.

The layer of moss covered the ground like a thick carpet under a fallen spruce tree. I pulled back large chunks of it until I had made a shallow nest. It was a little longer than the length of my body. The kidnappers were getting quite close as I wiggled in under the curve of the tree, and pulled a few clumps of the moss over me.

Any sound I could have heard was muffled. The heat and moisture of my own breath was loosening the dirt from the roots of the moss and sprinkling it onto my face and down my neck.

The ground vibrated with the group's footsteps and I knew they were getting close. My body sagged with relief when I realized they were walking on the other side of the fallen log. There was definitely no way they could see me. I sighed and let my head drop onto the damp earth.

A loud voice barked a quick command and the vibrations stopped. So did my breathing. All my senses were alive and tingling as I tried to hear, feel or smell anything that would tell me what they were doing. Fear took over for a moment as I realized they were going to make camp, no more than ten feet away from where I was lying.

It made no sense for them to camp here, in the bottom of a gully! Frost and fog always settles in the lowest areas first. Ancient people built tree forts to get up off the ground and out of the cold at night. If these kidnappers wanted to camp for the night in a blanket of cold frost they had picked the perfect place for it.

Brian's voice came to me first, then his mother's. It was easy to tell by her tone she wasn't happy. There were no other voices, but I knew the kidnappers couldn't be far away. Taking a few deep breaths to calm my racing heart, I braced my toes in the soft dirt and pushed myself ahead a few inches. The moss stayed with me, still covering most of my body.

My ears strained to hear any possible sound my movement had made or any change in the conversation from the other side of the log. There was none. I repeated the movement again until I reached a place where a dip in the ground had created a thin crack of airspace underneath the log. Digging slowly, scooping out one handful at a time, I made a tunnel under the log almost big enough for a cat to crawl through.

The sound of Brian's mother's voice carried through clearly and I could see a pair of pajamas. They were too big to be Brian's, so they must have belonged to his dad. Brian's mother wouldn't have been complaining so much if she thought the kidnappers could hear her. It stood to reason they were out of earshot from me as well.

It wasn't the perfect way for me to make contact with Brian. I really hoped neither Brian nor his mother would scream.

Hook

It was almost dark by the time they finally stopped. The sun had not gone down all the way, and the trees cast long shadows making it harder to see where they were walking.

The giant's face was red and sweaty. He dropped onto both knees and lay Keith, still drugged, on the ground. Both Brian and his mother rushed over to help. Brian's mother sat with her husband's head in her lap. Brian held his hand.

The three kidnappers were huddled together, several feet away, talking quietly over a map. Mr. Grumpy poked the map with his finger then pointed to a nearby hill. The driver shrugged his shoulders and started tapping the map. Mr. Grumpy grabbed the map and turned it 180 degrees.

Brian's feet were swollen, scratched and sore. "Great," he said. "The fashion boys from Black-R-Us don't have any idea where we are."

"I don't care where we are," his mother said. "I've been scared out of my wits for days. Now my feet are bleeding, *and* I am cold, *and* tired *and* hungry. If they are trying to kill us slowly they are doing a great job. The police will never be able to find the murder weapon either. I'll have a stroke; you'll starve to death, and your father . . . oh your poor father. I wish he would wake up so I could smack him."

"I know where we are," I whispered.

Brian's mother flinched hard and her eyes flew open but she never made a sound. Brian's head snapped up. While his mother complained, Brian had been staring at what looked like a strange pile of twigs. He had looked right at me but hadn't seen me. I slid my hand slowly along the ground and poked my fingers out from behind my hiding place.

"Either I'm loosing my mind from starvation, or my best friend's hand just grew out of a tree," Brian whispered. It made me smile. Then as casual as could be, he asked, "If you were just going to go popping up out of a log, why didn't you do it before they marched us halfway to Mexico? By the way, do you know what time it is?"

It seemed like a funny question, and I had to turn my head away so I wouldn't laugh out loud. This wasn't a good time for my friend to show his humorous side. "Yes, it's dusk," I said, turning back.

"Hey buddy!" he said. "Do you have your *watch on?*"

"Yes," I answered.

"Then how about going back to the van, and grabbing the voice transmitter out of my bag," Brian said as natural as could be. "You can put your watch battery in it and order me a pizza. While you're at it, you might want to call for backup. If it isn't too much to ask, tell the police to bring their guns."

Same old Brian, I thought. "I have the bag with me, and the police are already on their way. I'm not sure how far behind us they are. They might not be able to find us after dark."

"They can if you tell them where we are."

"The signal will never make it out of this gully, so as soon as it gets dark I'll go up to the top of this hill here and start signaling," I said.

"Don't forget the pizza, man."

"I don't have a pizza, but I can get you some mushrooms if you like."

"I only eat mushrooms on pizza. Besides, you can't eat mushrooms from the forest, they make you hallucinate and mess you up," he said.

This gave me an idea.

The kidnappers had started to move around again, so our conversation ended. The fellow with square-toed boots came over and, much to Mrs. Lutz's annoyance gave Mr. Lutz another shot to keep him sleeping. Two of the kidnappers found places to curl up and sleep, while the third kept watch.

As I had hoped, the third guard moved to where they had entered the gully so he could watch the trail. Unless he turned around, I'd be completely out of his line of sight.

The night was extra cold in the small gully. There was a full moon in the sky. I knew from experience that the full moon is the coldest night of the month. There were a few clouds.

Just as when I turn out the light in my room at night, it took a little while for my eyes to adjust. At first it was complete black, and I couldn't see a thing. I watched the cloud begin to move in, and tucked my head down to block out the moon's light. When the clouds started to cover the moon I started to move. The kidnapper's eyes would not have adjusted fully to the lower light yet; it would have been harder for him to see me crawling silently up the hill.

Trying to stay as low as possible, I dragged the backpack behind me as I began to crawl up the hill. At the top, I pulled the ball cap out of the bag and waited for the moon to come back out from behind the clouds. It didn't take very long, and I set to work.

Using my teeth to get the back off my watch, I worked the battery free. Unfolding the seam of the ball cap, I found the battery pouch and exchanged a dead battery for my good one. If the hat usually took four or five batteries, and only lasted a few hours, I knew adding only one good battery would only make it work for a few minutes.

I held it in my hands and talked into it, hoping someone (Mom) would hear. "Contact," I said. "I have made contact with the family. They're all alive. Mr. Lutz is being kept asleep by some drug and the kidnappers are lost. There are three of them, and they all have guns."

I've always had a good sense of direction in the woods, from hanging around Dad. I gave the best directions I could on how to find us. I told them all the landmarks that might help, repeating the message several times. When the battery was dead, I put the hat back in the bag and got to work finding breakfast. If Brian and I were hungry, the kidnappers must also be thinking to fill their bellies. I was going to help them do just that.

I scanned the woods for the glowing white of a birch tree at night. This time of year chanterelles were usually found underneath them. The moonlight wasn't bright enough to tell the difference between the false and true chanterelle. It didn't matter though, because I knew I had a bunch of safe mushrooms in the backpack already. I found a patch of them and picked every last mushroom.

You usually find a mushroom Dad calls "fly agaric," under birch trees as well. My whole life I had been taught to avoid these small reddish-orange mushrooms with little white flecks. I had been told the story of how the Sami people of Lapland would use these mushrooms to round up their reindeer herds.

Reindeer liked the flavour of the fly agaric, and the Sami people would pick the mushrooms and dry them. When they wanted to round up the herds they would scatter the mushrooms for the herd to eat. The mushroom makes you see things aren't there, and feel light-headed and fuzzy for about twelve hours. More than enough time to get the reindeer *happily* rounded up, without anyone getting kicked, trampled or gouged by antlers.

In a moment of inspiration, I grabbed a handful of the poisonous mushrooms. I opened the front pouch of the bag to put the new mushrooms inside, but separate from the ones I had picked earlier in the day.

The front pouch contained Brian's pencil case. I pulled it out and opened it to find what I knew would be there. All three corners had been snapped off, but would still work. Grabbing the backpack, I headed down the far side of the hill, away from the gully.

The *Junior Woodchuck Manual* says,
Birch trees liked it dry, So they stayed up high.
Willows like it wet, So they stay low, you bet.'
Red willow trees have a thin layer of stringy fibers under the bark. These can be used to help you relax, or put you to sleep. The trick is not getting any of the outside bark because it tastes so bad.

I ran along the bottom of the hill until I found the right kind of tree, thinking this would have been so much easier in the daylight. I took the metal compass and opened it as wide as I could and started to work.

Digging the pointy end into the bark, and wiggling it helped loosen the outer layer. I did this many times, making a rectangle set of holes in the bark. I used my fingers to get started at the top: the rectangle of holes acted like the perforated edge on postage stamps and the bark ripped cleanly along the lines.

Using the sharp edge of the triangle, I scrapped the little red fibers off both the bare tree trunk and the underside of the bark in my hand. I sprinkled the fibers onto the mushroom mixture and tossed it all together like a salad. Then I zipped the bag back up, made a mental note *not* to lick my fingers, and headed back to the gully.

Waiting for cloud cover, I slipped back behind the fallen spruce tree. Brian and his mother were huddled together, trying to stay warm. The fog had started to gather. With only pajamas to protect them from the cold, I doubted they would be able to asleep.

Brian lay down with his head in front of the hole when he heard my whisper. We talked until we had come up with a plan. We wished each other luck and I slid the mushrooms under the log. One pile at a time, so he could keep them separate.

In the super dark of pre-dawn I crawled back up the hill to wait for Brian and his kidnappers' first movements. I didn't want to get caught. Unfortunately, it was my father's angry face that greeted me at the top of the hill. For a brief moment I wondered where I would be safer. Up here with him, or down there with the kidnappers.

Line

Dad and I walked quickly down the other side of the rise. Once we were a safe distance away from the kidnappers we started to talk. Not angry father to guilty son, but like two people on the same team. I knew he was mad because I had left the car without telling them where I was going, or why, but he knew it wasn't the time for him to stay angry right now.

He informed me that although we had walked for a long time, the kidnappers really weren't very far from where they had started and the police teams were closer than I thought. I read in a magazine once about how the military did tests on some of its soldiers. They took them to the desert and told them to walk in a straight line. They always walked in a circle. Eighty percent walked in a circle to the left and the rest went to the right. The lead kidnapper had done the same thing.

The reason for this is because no one's legs are exactly the same size. Most people's right leg is longer, and stronger, than their left, which means their left leg will make shorter strides than their right. If one side of your body is going faster and further than the other, you will automatically walk in a circle. FACT.

I told Dad about the plan Brian and I had worked out. When I finished, he picked up the cellphone. With the first half smile I had seen in days, Dad told the police teams what to look for and what to expect. Then, hanging up the phone, he asked me when I had last had something to drink.

Dad and I had been having tea breaks, for as long as I can remember; we called it having "tree tea." With his army knife, Dad started to cut a good size "V" in the side of a maple tree. It works with any tree, but we always picked maples.

Smiling smugly at him I did the same thing, but with my metal protractor. Then, using my plastic triangle, I lifted the bark at the bottom of the V by about an inch. The lip was just big enough to put the lid off the plastic pencil case under the flap of bark. The bark pressed back down and held the lid in place the way a can opener does.

A big grin spread across my father's face as he watched what I had done. I dumped the pencils out and I handed him the bottom part of the case, to use as well. In a few minutes we where having our first sip of tree tea.

"About all the stuff you're going to feed those poor guys down there. First of all, this is about the only time I can imagine I wouldn't get mad at you for doing it. Secondly, I'm proud of you for thinking it up. Maybe you do listen to old Dad sometimes!

"Your mother was out of her mind with worry when you disappeared. I would like to say you should have waited for the rest of us, but I'd be wrong. You've done the right thing exactly when it should have been done all through this whole ordeal.

"However, you need to remember there are six other guys and me here to help make this happen. I don't want to see any stupid hero tactics from you as the day goes on. You hear me?"

"I hear you," I said. We sat in our usual friendly silence, drank tree tea and waited for the action to start. It didn't take long.

And Sinker

Brian had been busy back in the gully. Once everyone started moving around again, he asked to go to the bathroom. They let him go, with the strict order not to get out of sight. He obeyed, but took his time on purpose. According to plan, Brian bent down as if collecting something from the forest floor.

When he was seated once again beside the log, he pulled out his two piles of goodies. Andrew had told him the mushrooms were going to be two different colours. The difference still surprised him.

Brian divided up the pile of safe mushrooms for him and his mother. His dad still lay white and unconscious. The mixture of bad mushrooms sat in a separate pile in front of him. The little red fibers looked like they had come from the mushrooms themselves.

As planned, Brian and his mother nibbled at the mushrooms until the kidnappers noticed what they were doing. The giant was the first to pay attention and came over to see what they had. Brian tried hard not to sound too eager as he told the giant they were wild mushrooms he had found. Now that the eating had caught the kidnappers' attention, Brian and his mother began to eagerly eat their safe ones.

"Are they poisonous?" the giant asked.

Brian raised an eyebrow. "Were you never a Boy Scout? Can't you tell a bad mushroom from a good one?" Brian and his mother put the last of the safe mushrooms into their mouths and started chewing.

"No kid," said the giant a little annoyed. "They do not have that many wild mushrooms growing in Chicago. Mind if I help myself?"

He wasn't really asking; he bent down and scooped up most of the red pile. The pile was meant for the three of them and Brian wasn't sure what would happen if this guy ate them all. The giant was the nicest of the bunch and Brian didn't wish him any real harm. The giant went over to the others, and shared.

"Hey kid," called the new guy. "Get out there and pick some more of those."

Brian didn't have the first idea what to pick, or where to even look for mushrooms. "I picked the whole patch," he said quickly.

The driver stared at him for a few seconds, then ordered him to get up so they could get moving. The giant returned to where they were seated and did a few quick stretches before he grabbed Brian's dad and lifted him onto his shoulder. This time, the giant's face showed signs of pain. His muscles must have been tired from the efforts of carrying Brian's dad all day yesterday.

Once again they were placed in single file, and started off. This time Brian knew Andrew was out there somewhere beside him. He was watching for a sign both he and Andrew knew would be coming soon. What Brian did not know was that six policemen and Andrew's dad were also watching for the same sign.

The first ingredient from the mushroom salad that would affect the kidnappers would be the fibers of red willow bark. The kidnappers would probably think that their lightheaded feeling was coming from not having anything to eat in a whole day.

At first they might notice the tingling in their fingers, toes and probably even the tips of their noses. They might think it was from sleeping on the hard ground, in the damp fog. The soft fuzzy feeling would spread over them, inch by inch.

There was only one kidnapper walking in front of Brian. Brian watched him carefully for the first sign that the mushrooms were taking effect. The driver was carrying his gun in the ready-to-fire position as he had done yesterday.

Brian watched with increasing fear and nervousness as the driver started to clench and unclench his left hand. He shook it a few times trying to get the blood circulating. The feeling must have spread into his right hand, as well, because the driver took his gun and slung it over his shoulder so he could rub his hands together.

By now the false chanterelles should start giving them all mild gas pains. Nothing out of the ordinary, so they still would not be too alarmed. Brian couldn't see what was happening to the two kidnappers behind him. He chanced a glance back.

The giant was still red-faced from the effort of carrying his dad. He was walking further behind than he had been at any time yesterday. He wouldn't have been able to hear the other kidnappers complaining about the numbness or any other strange symptoms they were experiencing.

Mr. Grumpy wasn't showing signs of anything other than being annoyed. His lips were pressed together as tightly as his eyebrows were. This fellow, Brian knew without a doubt, was the one to be most afraid of.

The pace had slowed a little — a relief to Brian's bare feet. They were more swollen this morning than they had been the night before. Come on feet, he told himself. Just carry me through the next few minutes and I'll let you rest.

The driver stopped dead in his tracks. Without saying anything, Brian and his mother also stopped. They knew the false chanterelles were taking effect. Brian's mind began to race. His nerves were twitching and he was ready to spring. The driver started moving again, shaking his head, trying to clear it. For the second time, he moved his gun to his back so that it hung by its strap over his shoulder. He rubbed his hands together vigorously, then started rubbing his arms.

In minutes this would all be over. The dice had been tossed, and the game was about to end.

Trapped

The powerful stuff was kicking in. The fly agaric mushrooms were the toughest of the bunch and would take the longest to be absorbed by the body. They were starting to tell the kidnapper's brains to relax and not worry so much. This new relaxed state would slow the reflexes of all three men, giving Brian and his mother an advantage. Their moment of action could be now.

The driver stopped again and turned to the rest of the group. "You keep going, I'll catch up with you in a minute. I need a few minutes to myself."

"No," responded Mr. Grumpy, still looking angry. "We're not splitting up. You go do what you need to." He pointed his gun at the giant who had fallen behind. "It'll give *him* time to catch up."

The driver walked a short way into the woods, shaking his head. Puffing hard, the giant finally caught up, and dropped Brian's father to the ground. He took a few steps away and sat down with his head between his legs to catch his breath.

Now was the time for action. Brian looked at his mother. Taking a deep breath, and begging his feet to ignore the pain in them for the next few minutes, Brian started running as fast as he could in the opposite direction of the driver.

Again and again he chanted to himself the most important words he had ever heard in his life. The giant had said, they didn't kill people, they were "just a delivery service". The words pulsed through Brian's brain as his feet, searing with the pain of a thousand cuts, slipped and slid their way further into the woods.

The mushroom mixture was starting to have its full effect and when Brian took off, it took the new guy a few seconds to realize what was happening. Picking his gun up off the ground, he turned to face the direction Brian had gone. He brought the gun up to his shoulder adjusting the sights to the middle of Brian's back. Then lowering the sights slightly, he squeezed the trigger.

Brian was running in a straight line, because he knew he needed to put as much distance as possible between himself and the kidnappers. It could gain him some much needed distance.

The first rifle fire sounded like a firecracker going off a few feet behind him. He could feel the sound deep in his chest. Instinct told him to duck low and keep running. He changed his plan and now he was running in a zigzag pattern.

Before the echo from the first shot had time to bounce off the nearby mountains, a second, third and fourth shot rang out into space behind him. Above the gunfire the giant's huge voice bellowed a sonic wave of anger. It settled in Brian's chest and echoed all around him as he threw himself deeper into the forest.

Branches whipped past Brian's face. He barely had time to throw his hand up in front of himself to ward off a blow before a second branch came smashing toward him. Brian stumbled and tripped through the dense underbrush. He had to draw the kidnappers away from his father.

Mr. Grumpy was running after him, firing in his direction. The giant had left his heavy baggage and thought it would be easy to overtake a barefooted teenager. If he had had a clear mind the distance between them would have closed quickly. But no matter how hard he shook his head he couldn't clear it or get his limbs to move faster.

The second the giant started moving, Brian's mother leapt to her feet and tried to grab her husband. He was far too heavy for her to lift so she wrapped her arms around his chest and started dragging him back down the trail the way they had come. Her hands slipped and she had to adjust them again to get a better hold.

She knew this was her only chance to save his life. Her body responded, finding the extra strength to pull him away.

At the first sign of Brian making a move, Dad and I started running. I could hear my father calling for me to stay low. He swiped at my hand, but I refused to give in. In an unexplainable flash, I knew where I needed to be; and I was going.

Without looking back, Brian knew someone was gaining on him. His pulse was hammering in his ears. Something warm and wet was moving down his right cheek. Heavy footsteps were coming up from somewhere behind him. Closer and closer the pounding footsteps came.

The footsteps were only a few feet away when Brian tried to dive to the left. It was too late. A powerful hand clamped down on his shoulder. It dragged him to his knees and finally into a face first slide over the rough forest floor.

I could see two police officers charging through the woods. They had fired their guns into the air to try to draw the attention of the only functioning kidnapper. The mushrooms seemed to have had no effect on him whatsoever.

He had leveled his gun at Brian and missed. Then he started running. I was running too, because I knew what the kidnapper knew. In forest this dense, and with a moving target, he had to get closer if he was going to get a clean shot.

Dad and I had been higher up than the kidnappers when it started. We had the advantage of running downhill. Dad was no longer following me; he had taken a path of his own. Brian was no longer moving in a straight line and it was harder to tell where he was headed.

The man in black slowed his pace and again brought his gun in front of him. He wouldn't shoot if he didn't have a clear shot at Brian, and I wasn't going to let it happen.

I jumped, as Dad threw his army knife. Both Dad and I found our targets. I grabbed Brian's shoulder and we rocketed to the ground. The shot never went off. Dad's knife stuck deep into the trigger hand of the shooter. He dropped the gun and turned with surprise to see my father and two police officers moving toward him.

It had been agreed Dad and I would try to get to the family and the three teams of police officers would try to take out the boys in black. In a split-second decision we had both decided Brian looked as if he needed the most help. The police officers had their handguns leveled at the injured kidnapper and were in control. He was no longer a threat.

Brian thrashed his arm backward at me as I started to pick myself up. I reached out and took the swinging arm and started to help him. Only then did I realize that he had no idea who had knocked him down.

"Make sure he's all right," Dad said pointing at Brian's face. "I'm heading back to find the others." He disappeared at a dead run.

"My folks!" Brian yelled, pushing me off and starting after my father. "Did they get away?"

"I don't know," I told him. "Two of the boys in black started after you so both Dad and I took off after you, too. Your mother was left alone for at least a few minutes. I hope it was long enough!" There was no point in saying 'come on let's go,' because Brian was already trying to catch up with my dad.

Dad found Brian's mom sitting alone on a rock, trying to smooth her tangled hair, and wiping some of the dirt from her nightgown. Dad asked where her husband was, but she held her head high and refused to say.

"I buried him someplace safe," she said. "I'm not telling anybody where he is until you can prove to me all the kidnappers have been caught. He is safe where he is and he can darn well stay there."

Dad stood silently for a few seconds, then pulled his sweater over his head and offered it to her. When she reached out to take it, Dad stepped a little closer. "Oh Marion, look at your hands. Here, let my wipe you off a little."

He was looking at the dirt she had on her. If she had buried her husbandunder heavy moss or soft mud, Keith might suffocate. There was no sign of either. A small piece of a pine needle was stuck into her palm. She had simply piled brush over top of him. He would be fine, wherever he was, for a little while.

Brian and I arrived as Dad finished wiping off as much dirt as possible. He helped Mrs. Lutz into his sweater and asked her if it was all right for him to sit beside her

"Where's Dad?" Brian asked anxiously.

My father held up one hand. "Your mother did her job. She wants us to wait, so that's just what we're going to do."

By the time the second team of police officers reached the giant, he was sitting peacefully on the ground, with a happy smile on his face. They approached carefully even though he was holding himself up with his elbow resting on the butt of his gun. He had turned it upside down and driven the barrel end into the dirt. Realizing his limbs were not going to obey him, the giant's foggy brain had decided it was best to sit down and relax. It occurred to him that 'all that running around' didn't seem 'all that important' anymore.

The third police team had found the driver in much the same state; happy, quiet and a little confused. Much like the reindeer, both the driver and the giant were easily herded toward the road and the awaiting police cars. The new guy took another few minutes before the mushrooms really started having any effect on him.

"Some people have slower metabolisms," Dad explained. "Drugs take longer to affect them. This angry fellow must be one of them."

Once they had all been handcuffed and were safely headed toward the waiting police cars, an officer approached us. "They've all been taken care of," he said, very matter of factly.

"Are you sure there are no more of them?" asked Mrs. Lutz.

"No," he reassured her. "There are no more of them. We seem to be missing some of you, though! Where is your husband?"

"Over there behind the mossy rock," she answered pointing to a large boulder, about fifty feet away. Brian and I followed the path of her finger and sure enough, there he was, under a pile of branches, loose dirt and rotting leaves. One of the police officers came over and helped us finish digging him out. His skin was damp and a creepy colour of white.

"The kidnappers carried him into the woods, so I guess we'll have to carry him out," said Dad. He started to pick Keith up by the armpits. Brian stepped forwards, to pick up his father's feet, but the police officer cut him off and gently moved Brian to the side.

"Son," he said with a grim smile. "I'll take your dad. From the looks of you, I think you will be doing a fine job carrying yourself out of the woods. How are you holding up anyway?"

"Me?" he said sounding surprised. "I'm fine, I guess. My life has turned into an Arnold Schwartzenegger movie. Rocketing around in speeding cars, being chased, things blowing up, hiding and seeking. It looks like so much fun in the movies, but in real life . . . Man! It *Sucks*! I haven't eaten in two days. I've walked halfway to Mexico, I'm sure. I have a broken nose from my *friend* jumping me, a fat lip, a cut cheek and feet that look like I put them through a blender. All in all, I'd say I'd rather have been in math class!"

"Not in those jammies," I laughed. "It scares me to think where you shop, buddy!"

"Look, I've had a bad day, man," he said. "Do you think you could cut me a little slack?"

"Batman! How uncool is that?" I teased. "I didn't know they even made Batman pajamas that big! Now if it had been Spiderman . . . well then, I would have understood. Spiderman way out-cools Batman."

"They were a present. I didn't get to pick them out. Besides, I'm freezing. Give me some of your clothes, and at least one of your sneakers so I can hop out of here. My feet are killing me."

We joked our way back to the cars. Everything seemed extra funny and tears of laughter rolled down our cheeks. It ended when I saw my mother. I knew from the look in her eyes, just before she hugged every breath of air out of me, we were going to have a long talk at the kitchen table about obeying.

The Aftermath

The Lutz family spent the first day in the hospital being checked out. Brian did break his nose after all, and Keith woke up with a huge headache. Other than that, everyone was fine. The next day, they moved into our house . . . along with an armed guard.

Mom had our house wired like Fort Knox. I think, in a way, it was fun for her. For the first time ever Dad and I didn't complain about all the *"little presents"* left around the house by the Radio Shack Fairy. She opened up her tickle trunk of toys and set them all up. She even wired the lawn with vibration sensors. If anything bigger than a cat walked anywhere on our property, it would set off the alarm.

One night at supper Mrs. Lutz asked, "What ever happened to the fourth guy? The one who drove the other van, with Keith in it. Did we ever find him?"

"Yes," said Dad. "One of the police teams saw a stranger walking down the road in the middle of nowhere. When they pulled over to talk to him he tried to pretend he was from around here, but he was dressed in all black and it gave him away. No one wears all black around here.

"Someone must have forgotten to tell them that, in the country, everyone ends up dressing like their tractors. If a guy owns a John Deere, he wears a green hat. It might have worked if someone sold black tractors but they don't.

"This guy stuck out like a flag. They asked for some ID but he said he didn't have any on him, so they brought him in. The police told him he could go as soon as he could prove who he was. US officials are on their way to pick him up."

While we were talking, one of the yard alarms went off. The chime of our front door bell quickly drowned out the ringing. Mom got up to answer it. She returned with a person wearing a straight black suit, plain glasses and very short brown hair. I stared at this new guest, as we all stood to say hello. I would have said, "Hello, ma'am," or "Hello, sir" but I couldn't say for sure if it was a he, or a she. The voice was halfway between a younger man with a soft voice, and a woman with a slightly husky voice.

Keith knew who it was right away and came across the room to offer his hand and say hello. The handshake made me think it must be a man. Keith introduced everyone to his main contact at the Witness Protection Program, Pat Charlton. The name didn't give me any clues either. Pat could be a girl or a boy, but at least Pat smiled.

Once we were seated, Pat turned to Keith and asked what he remembered. This was the first time I had heard anyone ask Keith for his side of the story. He said it was not nearly as exciting as ours because if he started to wake up, they gave him another shot and off to sleep he went. He woke up twice at the cabin, to eat and go to the bathroom. He laughed. "I can't tell you what it was I ate."

Pat smiled for only a second, then looked at all the Lutzs. "I can't even begin to tell you how sorry we all are this happened. We had no idea there was an informant in our agency. If it had not been for your family and your friends, here, we would have never caught him. Once again, Keith, the agency thanks you."

"I had nothing to do with it," Keith said. "I just slept. These boys did most of it."

Pat turned toward Brian. "We have a lot to thank you for, and a lot to make up for. If you have any special requests, I'd be more than happy to pass them on to my bosses."

"I don't want to move again," Brian said flatly.

Holding his gaze, Pat said, "You won't have to."

"But our house is gone, isn't it?" Brian asked. "They told me it was destroyed."

Still staring directly at Brian, Pat reached out his/her closed fist. Pat moved the fist over to Brian, inches away from his chest. Brian looked back and forth between the closed fist and Pat's face several times, not understanding. Slowly Pat turned the fist palm up and began opening the fingers.

"We always pay for our mistakes," Pat said slowly, staring hard at Brian. "These are keys to your new home. It's down the street, if you want to go look at it. It's completely empty, so we've put some startup money in your account, for you to buy your own furniture . . . and pajamas, this time."

"I don't want you to buy me any new clothes," Brian countered, holding his gaze.

"But I thought you'd like Batman pajamas," Pat said with a crooked smile. "Batman was my favourite when I was young."

"And exactly how many years did you spend in therapy?"

"How can we stay here if the mob already knows were we live?" Keith interrupted.

"They don't know where you live," Pat answered. "They had an informant but he never contacted them directly. He hired the kidnappers himself — using agency money, by the way. He was supposed to deliver you back to Chicago.

"The kidnappers can't say anything, to anyone, because they're all in jail. As for the informant, who you so helpfully found for us, he's locked up so tight and has so many other things to worry about right now, that where we moved you to this time will be the last thing on his mind. Besides, we never let people stay in the same place after there's been any kind of leak and he knows it. The last place he'd tell them to look is right here."

"I guess the best place to hide a tree is in the forest," said Keith.

Brian's mom spoke up for the first time as she reached for the house keys, which were still in Pat's hand. "I think I have had enough of trees for quite some time, thank you." Then she turned to the rest of us with a smile. "Come on neighbours, let's go look at our new house!"

ABOUT THE AUTHOR

Allison Maher was a former manager
of a company that invented "spy gear".
She now lives on a small farm in rural
Nova Scotia. *I, The Spy* is her first
juvenile novel.